# MONSTERSTREET
## CAMP OF NO RETURN

**4**

# MONSTERSTREET

## CAMP OF NO RETURN

# J. H. REYNOLDS

KATHERINE TEGEN BOOKS
An Imprint of HarperCollins Publishers

Katherine Tegen Books is an imprint of
HarperCollins Publishers.

Monsterstreet #4: Camp of No Return
www.harpercollinschildrens.com
Library of Congress Control Number: 2019957927
ISBN 978-0-06-286944-9 (trade)
ISBN 978-0-06-286943-2 (pbk.)

Typography by Ray Shappell
20 21 22 23 24   PC/BRR   10 9 8 7 6 5 4 3 2 1
❖
First Edition
Also available in a hardcover edition.

For Rosemary Stimola and Ben Rosenthal,
who made my dreams come true

# 1

# THE LUCKY ONES

Harper peered out the window of the bus at the thick gray fog. It had been following them the entire drive. She watched the pine trees pass in the mist like phantoms, thinking it felt more like Halloween outside than the week after Fourth of July.

*I hope the weather clears up*, she thought. *Otherwise my one chance to go to Camp Moon Lake is going to be ruined!*

She glanced around the bus at all the jittery campers. A group of boys nearby were shooting spitballs through straws, and the girls across the aisle were shouting at them to stop. Most of the other kids were playing games or taking selfies with their smartphones.

There wasn't a single empty seat. Harper had to take the very last one in the back of the bus after her parents had been late dropping her off in town. And they were late for the same reason they were always late. . . .

They had been arguing.

Again.

Even worse, they had told her that her going away to camp would give them some time to "figure things out." She was pretty sure she knew what that meant. Her friend Josie's parents had said the same thing last year. And now they lived in different houses, basically on two different planets, with Josie having to go back and forth every other weekend. Josie had told Harper that the divorce felt like she had been abducted from the home she'd always known and that she hadn't had a good night's sleep since.

Needless to say, Harper was afraid the same

thing would happen to her as soon as camp was over.

"Have you ever been to Camp Moon Lake before?" the girl sitting next to Harper asked. She looked about nine—a few years younger than Harper—and was wearing pink bows in her pigtails.

"No. First time," Harper answered, noticing that the thick lenses of the girl's glasses made her eyes look twice as big as they actually were.

"I can't believe I got in," the girl said. "My cousin has applied every summer for the past five years and never made it past the first round of the lottery. She said it's the hardest summer camp in the world to get into."

"When you really think about it, it does sort of feel like we won the golden ticket to Willy Wonka's Chocolate Factory," Harper mused aloud.

"Exactly!" the girl replied, then paused. "I—I am kind of nervous, though. I've never stayed away from my parents overnight before."

"There's nothing to worry about," Harper

said, encouraging her. "Besides, you've already made one friend."

The girl looked up at Harper and smiled.

"Thanks," the girl said. "I'm Darla."

"I'm Harper."

"It's nice to meet you," Darla replied. "So what do you think we'll be doing all week? Everything's so top secret. I mean, my parents had to sign a form that promised I wouldn't ever tell anyone what happens at camp—including them."

"Mine too," Harper said, pushing a strand of her dark hair behind her ear. "I was surprised they signed it. But they were so excited that I had actually gotten in, they didn't seem to mind. We must be doing really fun, out-of-this-world stuff, because the welcome letter said, 'We GUARANTEE that Camp Moon Lake will be the best week of your life!'"

Just then, the boy sitting in front of them turned around. He had been writing in his notepad the entire drive but apparently had also been eavesdropping on Harper and Darla's conversation.

"My neighbor told me something about why the camp is so secretive," he said softly, taking a puff from his inhaler. His pale skin made him look like he hadn't seen the sun all summer.

"What did your neighbor say?" Harper asked, thinking the boy reminded her of Edward Scissorhands.

The boy glanced over his shoulder to make sure no one else was listening.

"Just that a bunch of kids were murdered at Camp Moon Lake a few years ago. But there was a giant cover-up so that the camp's reputation wouldn't be tainted and parents would still let their kids keep coming here."

"Your neighbor probably made that up," Harper said, unsure if she could trust the boy.

"I don't think so. He said it was a bloodbath. But they never found any of the bodies. Just the blood."

"Camp Moon Lake is supposed to be the most magical summer camp on earth," Darla said, confused. "It says so in the brochure."

"And you're just going to take the brochure's word for it?" the boy asked, challenging her.

Darla was silent. She looked a bit horrified.

The boy took another puff from his inhaler.

"So you're telling us that someone was going around killing people with an ax or something and dragging their bodies off into the woods?" Harper questioned.

The boy shrugged. "Maybe. All I know is, I looked up the camp online, and there's mostly all new staff this year. Even weirder, there's absolutely no info about what goes on here. I mean, at some point through the years, some kid would have spilled the beans. But for some reason, they haven't. Or their tracks have been covered. And come to think of it, I've never actually met anyone who's been to Camp Moon Lake, have you?"

"If you really think that people were murdered here, then why did you come?" Harper asked.

"My parents made me," he replied. "They said any kid in the world should be doing backflips to get to go to Camp Moon Lake and that I was one of the 'Lucky Ones.' Whatever that means."

*He's right*, Harper thought. *No one in their right mind would turn down an invitation to come to Camp Moon Lake.*

Still unsure, Harper gestured to the boy's notepad. "Are you doing homework for summer school or something?"

"Oh, this?" he said. "It's just a new story I'm working on. I'm going to write books for a living when I grow up. Scary ones sell the best, so that's probably what I'm going for. I'm Brodie, by the way."

"I'm Harper. And this is Darla."

Harper gave a wave, deciding the boy had made up the story about the camp murders and was just trying to scare her and Darla.

It was then that Harper noticed something enormous looming out the front window of the bus.

A giant wooden sign. Held up by two massive pillars.

The sign read:

**WELCOME TO CAMP MOON LAKE
THE MOST MAGICAL SUMMER CAMP ON EARTH**

As the bus drove beneath it, the fog swirled around the pillars. For a moment, Harper thought they were made of gold, but she decided it must have been the way the wood looked in the mist.

*Wow*, she thought. *If the entrance is that fancy, then what's the rest of the camp going to be like?*

A few moments later, the bus stopped in the middle of the campground next to several wooded trailheads. All the kids, including Harper, pressed their hands and faces against the windows trying to capture their first glimpse of Camp Moon Lake. But it was too misty to see anything.

The bus driver called over the speakers, "Looks like fog is in the forecast for the rest of the week. We get a lot of it from the coast this time of year. Best if you all stick together when you're walking around the campground so you don't get lost."

He pulled his hat lower over his eyes, then he stepped off the bus and disappeared into the mist.

Harper didn't know why—maybe it was Brodie's story or the fact that she was feeling cold in the middle of summer—but the fog gave her an unsettled feeling, like it was hiding something.

Something dark.

And unfriendly.

And that's when she saw a girl run out of the mist covered in blood, screaming for her life.

# 2

# THE GRAND TOUR

**H**arper's stomach tightened into knots.

The girl's face and hair were drenched with blood. Her arms and legs were gashed up, with crimson fluid dripping down her skin. Even her shirt and shorts were soaked dark red.

But worst of all was the desperate, panicked look in the girl's eyes—like she knew she was about to die.

*If I go out there to help her, whatever got her will get me too,* Harper thought, debating whether to stay on the bus or aid the girl.

Harper hurried toward the front of the bus

to assist the ravaged victim but stopped when she heard a loud clattering below.

*Whatever's out there is trying to come in through the luggage compartment!* she thought in dread, deciding she should close the door to the bus.

Then . . .

Harper heard the girl yell from outside.

"Food fight!"

Harper saw several other girls and boys chasing after each other. Throwing food.

And that's when she realized the girl wasn't covered in blood.

She was drenched in . . .

*Ketchup!* Harper thought, feeling incredibly silly.

She watched as the kids disappeared behind a nearby cabin, their laughter echoing across the campground.

"This camp is going to be awesome!" Darla said, excited by the food fight.

A moment later, a redheaded woman with a whistle around her neck stepped onto the bus.

She was wearing a slime-green hat with the yellow camp logo on it, and her socks were pulled up to her knees. The driver lagged behind her and sat back down in his seat.

"Hi, kids! Welcome to Camp Moon Lake— the most magical summer camp on earth! I'm Counselor Fuller, and I'm thrilled to get to spend this week with you all," the woman at the front of the bus said. She had a warm, soothing voice, and her smile made Harper feel immediately welcomed. "As you just saw, the campers who arrived this morning are finishing up their afternoon food fight. That said, we have a lot of exciting things planned this week. Follow me, and I'll give you the grand tour! But first, I need to take your cell phones."

"How come?" asked a tall girl at the front of the bus. Harper had noticed her posting pictures on her Instagram account during the drive. The name tag beneath her long brown hair read, *Regina*. The girl sitting next to her was Tabitha. They looked like clones in their blue T-shirts and black gym shorts. Harper figured they were probably cheerleaders or something.

Counselor Fuller smiled patiently. The smile never seemed to leave her face.

"Camp policy," she replied. "We can't have photos of all the fun things we do getting out to the public, can we? It would take away from the same mystique that made you want to come here in the first place. Your parents are aware of this policy and have all signed release forms."

Brodie leaned over and whispered in Harper's ear, "Or they don't want any pictures of ax murderers getting out to the public."

Harper nudged him.

She, Brodie, and Darla followed the swarm of kids off the bus. Those like Harper who had phones reluctantly placed them in what looked like a miniature vault with a lock on it. The kids who weren't allowed or old enough to have phones yet—like Darla—went on their way, no better off or worse than before.

They waited while their bags were unloaded from the storage compartment under the bus.

As soon as Darla's suitcase hit the ground,

she reached for it but had trouble lifting it on her own.

"Here, I'll help you," Brodie offered, picking it up for her. "I have a little sister back home, so I'm used to it."

"Thanks," Darla said with a smile.

*Even if I can't trust Brodie, at least he's nice,* Harper thought, surprised by his act of kindness.

"Oh, don't worry about your luggage," Counselor Fuller called over to them from the entrance to a trailhead.

"You want us to just leave it here?" Harper asked.

"The camp valets will carry it to your cabins for you," Counselor Fuller replied.

*Camp valets?* Harper thought in astonishment. *Is this a summer camp for kids or a resort for the rich and famous?*

As they followed Counselor Fuller down the wooded trail, there were other grinning counselors at multiple snack stations handing out free snow cones to the new arrivals. Best of all, there wasn't even a line, and they had just enough of each flavor. It was almost as if they already knew which kind each kid would want.

While they walked, Brodie stared down at his purple, grape-flavored snow cone.

"This is probably gut juice," he said. "You know, from all the kids who have died here."

"You're ridiculous," Harper replied. "If anyone had actually died here, they would have closed down the camp for good. Besides, this place is like the Disney World of summer camps. It's too magical for anything bad to happen."

As they continued the grand tour, Counselor Fuller showed them the go-kart racing track, a multiloop roller coaster, stables with exotic animals like giraffes and zebras, and the outdoor movie theater where they could watch a new double feature every night. The marquee for the evening read, *"Back to the Future* and *The Goonies."* They even passed by a water park with its own wave pool, lazy river, bumper boats, and nexus of waterslides.

"This place is incredible!" Darla gushed.

"It's beyond anything I dreamed."

"Yeah," Harper agreed, hardly believing it herself. "It's pretty amazing."

Brodie took a puff from his inhaler and looked around, as if searching for clues. He seemed ultraparanoid, like a twelve-year-old Sherlock Holmes.

Nearby, a woman in a white dress waved to the campers as she walked into a giant black building. She looked older, like their grandparents' age, and she had a big smile on her face, just like the rest of the counselors.

"That's Nurse Betty," Counselor Fuller said, waving back. "She's been at Camp Moon Lake for a very long time. She'll take care of you if you get hurt or feel sick at any point during the week. Don't hesitate to pay her a visit in her office at the mess hall if you need anything."

"I'm sure I'll be spending a lot of time there," Brodie said, taking another puff from his inhaler. "Even though that's probably where they hide all the dead bodies. Just like in *The 'Burbs*."

Harper ignored him.

"My parents love old movies, so that's why I reference them all the time," Brodie added.

"It's kind of weird," Harper said, then continued walking.

Even though she couldn't see the horizon because of the fog, she sensed that the sun was setting because the world seemed to be getting a bit darker.

Counselor Fuller soon stopped beside the cove of the lake next to a sign that read *Ropes Course*.

There were all sorts of interesting structures and bridges scattered about the field near the cove, all made of what looked like telephone poles, rope nets, and railroad ties.

But there was one thing that stood out from everything else. A wooden ladder attached to a giant thick pole reached so high into the sky, the top of it was lost in the fog. For all Harper knew, it could have gone all the way up into outer space.

"Wow," Darla said with awe. "What's that?"

"The highest zip line in the world," Counselor Fuller revealed proudly. "The launching platform is at the very top of the support pole, about three hundred feet in the air, and the zip line runs across the entire lake."

Harper peered up, feeling a knot of nervousness form in her stomach at the thought of climbing that high, much less soaring over the water on a metal wire.

It was then she saw something that seemed out of place.

Something that turned her blood ice-cold.

Blocking off the entrance of the zip line were several ribbons of yellow caution tape.

The same kind used to mark off crime scenes.

And places where murders happened.

"See. I told you," she heard Brodie whisper in her ear. "This camp is a death trap."

## 3

# TRUST FALL

"What happened there?" Harper asked, expecting the worst.

"Oh, that," Counselor Fuller said, still smiling. "The zip line is blocked off because of the fog. We can't have campers near the water in these conditions. Safety is our priority here at Camp Moon Lake."

Harper felt relieved that there was a logical explanation and a bit silly for letting her imagination get the best of her.

Counselor Fuller continued to the center of the ropes course and stopped next to a small edifice the size of a refrigerator box. There were five steps leading to the top of it.

"This is a trust table. All of camp life is built on trust," Counselor Fuller began. "And it's our tradition here at Camp Moon Lake for each camper to participate in a trust fall upon arrival. Now, can anyone tell me what a tr—"

Before she could finish, her walkie-talkie buzzed, and she stepped off to the side to answer it. She whispered something to the person on the other end of the line, then hurried back to the campers.

"I'm sorry. I have to go help set up something for the Opening Night Campfire," she said. "Does anyone here know how to explain a trust fall to the rest of the group?"

Darla eagerly shot her hand up in the air. She jumped up and down with excitement. "I do, I do!"

Counselor Fuller grinned at Darla's enthusiasm and waved for her to come up to the trust table. She talked with Darla for a moment, giving her a few tips, then jogged away down the path from which they had come.

Darla climbed the steps and stood proudly atop the trust table like a magician on her stage.

She turned to the campers.

"My family did this on our vacation last summer," she began, not the least bit shy in front of a crowd. "I have five brothers and sisters, and my parents are always trying to find new bonding activities for us to do."

Nearby, Regina rolled her eyes and made a face like she was throwing up.

Darla continued. "The way it works is I'll stand up here and fall backward off the stage. And four of you will stand below with your arms locked to catch me. Make sense?"

The campers nodded in understanding.

"I'll go first. Who wants to catch me?"

"We will," Harper volunteered, pulling Brodie up to the base of the trust table.

"We'll do it too," Regina said, dragging Tabitha up to the front of the crowd. Regina seemed like the kind of girl who liked attention.

Harper and Brodie locked arms across from

each other, and Regina and Tabitha did the same. Darla stepped to the edge of the platform with her back to them.

"Okay, when I say 'ready,' you say, 'fall away,'" Darla instructed. She then knelt and whispered to Harper, "If anything happens to me, tell my family I love them."

Harper smiled. "You'll be fine. I promise we'll catch you."

Regina rolled her eyes and whispered something in Tabitha's ear.

Darla took a deep breath and called out, "Ready?"

Harper, Brodie, Regina, and Tabitha shouted back in unison, "Fall away!"

Darla carefully backed up, her heels hanging over the edge of the table. She closed her eyes, folded her arms across her chest like she was lying in a coffin, and relaxed her body.

Three . . .

Two . . .

One . . .

The other campers watched in suspense as

Darla fell backward off the table toward her trust partners.

Downward . . .

And downward . . .

But when her weight fell into the human net below, Regina's and Tabitha's arms broke apart, and Darla tumbled headfirst to the ground.

*BAM!*

Darla sat up and rubbed the back of her head.

Harper and Brodie knelt at her side and examined her. She had a small bump bubbling out from her skull.

Harper looked up at Regina accusingly. "Why did you do that?"

"Our hands slipped," Regina said. "She shouldn't have fallen so hard."

Harper glared at her.

Brodie gave Darla some water from his canteen.

Feeling like a protective older sister, Harper stood and faced Regina.

"You could have really hurt her," Harper said.

"It was a stupid exercise anyway," Regina replied, not seeming the least bit remorseful.

"What's wrong with you? You should tell her you're sorry," Harper said in a more challenging tone.

Regina stepped toward Harper.

"You better watch yourself," Regina threatened. "Or you might cause another accident. Wouldn't want *both* of you to end up in the camp graveyard."

"Summer camps don't have graveyards," Harper said.

"Sure they do. Every camp has one. Even Camp Moon Lake. But they keep it hidden so that the campers don't get freaked out."

"You're making that up," Harper challenged.

"Actually, she might be telling the truth," Brodie whispered in Harper's ear.

Harper shot him a sour look.

Regina took another step toward Harper, and Tabitha followed, attached at her hip. For a moment, it looked like Regina was going to push Harper.

"If you haven't figured it out yet," Regina began, then looked up at the sky as if someone, or something, was watching them. "This camp isn't like other camps. Camp Moon Lake is . . . different."

Harper knew Regina was just trying to scare them. But before Harper could say anything else, she felt a cold, slimy tentacle wrap around her ankle.

She looked down and saw the scariest creature she had ever seen in her entire life. . . .

# 4

# CAMPFIRE TALES

The creature tightened itself around Harper's ankle, cutting off her circulation.

And that's when she realized what the thing was. . . .

"Snake!" she shouted.

Instinctually, she kicked her leg, and the snake flew through the air and landed in the grass. She watched in horror as it slithered away into the nearby cove.

Harper breathed a sigh of relief.

"Don't be such a wimp. It's probably just as afraid of you as you are of it," Regina taunted.

Before Harper could say anything back, a whistle shrilled behind her.

She turned and saw a counselor coming toward them. "Time to head over to the Opening Night Campfire! It's starting to get dark, so here are some flashlights. Be sure to stay on the path!"

The counselor opened up a canvas bag and handed out green flashlights that had the yellow camp logo on them. She then pointed toward a nearby trailhead sign that read *Campfire Corner.*

Harper, Brodie, and Darla followed the mob of campers down the narrow path canopied by trees. Their beams of artificial light illuminated the mist, giving the evening a haunting ambience.

Soon, Harper could see the orange glow of firelight ahead. The flames danced in the deepening twilight.

After they arrived, Harper, Darla, and Brodie sat down together on a log. Darla started roasting marshmallows. The first one fell off her stick, but she managed to toast the second one to a golden crisp.

She motioned for Harper to hand her a graham cracker. Harper rummaged in the open box nearby and gave one to her. Darla cracked it in half, put a chocolate bar on one side, and squished the marshmallow between the crackers.

Then she took a big bite.

"I love s'mores," Darla said as if it was her first time to ever try one. Then she handed the stick to Harper.

"I think those girls are going to be a problem for us, but especially for Darla," Harper whispered to Brodie.

Brodie moved his wild black hair out of his face and glanced across the fire at Regina and Tabitha, who were pushing two younger kids out of their chairs so they could sit down.

"Yeah. I can't believe Regina broke the trust fall—she definitely did it on purpose," Brodie said. "Let me know if they give you any more trouble. I've watched *The Karate Kid* at least a hundred times and have just about mastered the crane kick. I sort of feel like we need to protect Darla. . . . Otherwise, no one else will."

"Yeah," Harper said, touched by Brodie's protective brotherly instincts. "You know, back on the bus I wasn't sure what to think about you. But . . . you're all right."

"No offense, but you still don't know me that well," Brodie said with a wink, then began spraying himself all over with mosquito repellent.

The smell was so strong, Harper had to hold her nose.

Right then, a loud drum began to boom in the darkness on the other side of the campfire. Into the firelight stepped a tall, skinny man wearing a goofy hat that was shaped like a giant hot dog. His face was painted with streaks of red that looked like blood.

"Good evening, campers!" he called out. He squeaked a rubber bike horn in the air like a circus clown. "My name is Bronson McGee the fifth! But you can call me Director McGee. I'm the director of Camp Moon Lake."

"Hi, Director McGee!" the campers shouted back in unison.

Director McGee smiled. "Congratulations on winning the lottery to get to come to camp! It truly is a once-in-a-lifetime experience. My family has run this place for five generations, and like always, we guarantee to make it the most unforgettable week of your life!"

The campers cheered again.

Director McGee waited for a moment, then waved his hands for the kids to quiet down. "Now, listen up. Before we begin our week of fun and games, it's important that you each learn the camp rules. Your counselors will go over the list with you in your cabins before lights-out tonight, but there's one rule we need to address here. Right now." He paused, removed his silly hat, then added solemnly, "It's a matter of life or death."

Harper felt a chill rush over her. It was the first serious tone a counselor had used since they had arrived.

Director McGee took a deep breath and peered into the eyes of each camper. When he looked at Harper, the hairs on her arms stood up. She wondered if he was about to reveal something about the camp murders.

"This is very serious," Director McGee said. "Too many campers have ignored this rule, even though we warn them to follow it on the first night of every camp week, just like we're warning you now."

He took another long, thoughtful breath and met the eyes of each camper once again.

"The most important rule at Camp Moon Lake is . . ." He stepped closer to the firelight, then finally whispered, "Stay away from the forbidden cove. No swimming. No canoeing. No zip-lining. It's far too dangerous in the fog."

He gestured behind him, and the campers eagerly shined their flashlights in the direction where he was pointing. The collective beams turned into a giant spotlight that illuminated the edge of the lake. Blanketed with mist.

Harper could barely see the zip-line platform

on the bank a hundred yards over from them.

"Why? What's in the cove?" Brodie asked.

Director McGee leaned down so that the firelight reflected in his eyes. He held his hot dog–themed hat at his side, and Harper thought that the red streaks on his face looked like someone, or something, had clawed his cheeks and forehead.

"We don't know," Director McGee confessed. "And technically, the question isn't what's *in* the cove. The question is what's beyond it."

All the campers exchanged frightened, confused looks.

Harper waited for Director McGee to say that he was only kidding, but his gaze remained solemn.

"What I can tell you is a story that's been passed down to counselors and campers for many summers. It was told to me by my grandfather, and it was told to him by his granddaddy.

"As the legend goes, a girl came to Camp Moon Lake a long time ago and was told the same rule you've been told tonight. But she didn't listen. Instead, she climbed up to the zip line platform and rode the wire into the fog. The wire hissed as she slid across it and disappeared into the mist. But some campers who saw her do it said there was never a scream. No sound of her dropping into the water. She simply . . . disappeared. They pulled the handle back to the platform, but there was no one on it. It was a like a fishhook that had been stripped of its bait. And she was never heard from again."

Out of the corner of her eye, Harper noticed Darla listening attentively.

"I thought this was supposed to be the most magical summer camp on earth?" Darla whispered.

"So we can't have fun on the lake because some stupid girl messed things up for the rest of us like fifty years ago or something?" Regina called out from her stolen seat.

"Tragic as it is, it's not that simple," Director McGee replied, disregarding Regina's lack of empathy. "You see, ever since the girl disappeared, no camper who's gone beyond the cove when it's foggy has ever come back. Not a single one. And on some nights, while lying in the cabins, campers say they can hear a scream coming from the lake—a collective scream that grows bigger and louder every summer with each kid that doesn't return. And it's believed to be the ghost of the girl who haunts the waters, and all her captives, waiting to take more campers."

There was dead silence.

Everyone around the campfire sat still and quiet.

Harper scooted closer to Brodie, and Darla moved closer to Harper.

Even though it was too foggy to see anything, Harper could hear the water lapping up against the muddy bank.

And then, in the distance just beyond the cove, she heard the most terrible sound she had ever heard. . . .

# 5

# DOUBLE FEATURE

The sound blared again.

And again.

Harper covered her ears, as did all the other campers.

It sounded like a shrieking choir of voices.

Each camper sat wide eyed, staring at one another to see if anyone else had heard it.

Harper felt a chill rush over her. It was like a ghost had licked her spine with its icy tongue.

Darla remained motionless beside her.

A few moments passed, and the scream came again. Only this time, it was in the fog right next to the campfire.

Everyone stood up, ready to run.

Then . . .

Counselor Fuller jumped out of the bushes and howled into a microphone hooked into a portable speaker. Her shriek multiplied into a dozen shrills, all layered with reverb. It was the same banshee cry the campers had heard coming from the cove.

She and Director McGee high-fived each other and laughed. Realizing they had been fooled, the campers all booed, half-relieved the story wasn't true, half-angry that they had fallen for the prank.

Director McGee put his hot-dog hat back on and turned to the campers. "Gotcha!"

The campers booed again.

*This must have been the "thing" Counselor Fuller had to go set up earlier*, Harper thought.

"What would Opening Night Campfire be like without a spooky story?" Director McGee joked. "The truth is, a girl really did disappear in the cove a long time ago, and her body was never found. So it really is important for you to follow the rules and stay away from the cove during the fog. Understand?"

The campers nodded obediently.

*I don't know what to believe,* Harper thought.

"On another note, this is my last week as camp director," Director McGee revealed. "I'm retiring on Friday as soon as the last bus leaves to transfer you guys back home, and Counselor Fuller will be taking over from there. So this is a bittersweet week for me, and I plan to make the most of it with all of you."

Counselor Fuller stepped to his side and rested her arm on his shoulder. Harper thought she saw a tear glimmering in Director McGee's eye.

"It also means I'll be playing twice as many pranks as usual!" he added with a chuckle. "Once you finish with your s'mores, we'll head on over to the outdoor movie theater. Even though it's foggy, we should still be able to see the glow of the screen. Oh, and we have popcorn, sodas, and candy waiting for you at the concession stands."

On their way over to watch the movie, Harper, Brodie, and Darla walked side by side, huddling together in the chilly night air.

"I could have told a scarier story than that," Brodie bragged to the girls. "The twist ending was too predictable. Director McGee should have thrown in a twist on the twist. That's the best way to surprise your audience."

"Well, it scared me," Darla said.

"Me too," Harper agreed.

"All I'm saying is my story about the camp murders was better."

Harper turned to Brodie. "I knew you made that up!"

Brodie tried to hide his smirk.

"I needed to test it out before putting it to paper. That's what real storytellers do."

Harper felt frustrated that she had been coaxed into believing something that wasn't true. Not just once but twice—and in one day! She wondered how many times in her life she had fallen for tricks like Brodie's and Director McGee's without realizing it.

Worst of all, she again wasn't sure if she could trust Brodie. She wasn't sure if she could trust anyone.

For some reason, the whole thing made her think of her parents. She thought of all the fun times they had shared. All the memories. And she wondered if they too were just illusions.

*No use in dwelling on it while I'm here,* she told herself as the campers around her sang songs, told jokes, and made up more spooky stories. *Besides, I'm one of the Lucky Ones—I'm here at the most magical summer camp on earth.*

But her luck was about to run out.

# 6

## CAMP GAMES

The next morning, all the campers and counselors met in the mess hall for breakfast. There were long tables set up like a buffet, filled with pancakes, waffles, bacon, sausage, syrup, toast, and every other breakfast food a kid could dream up.

Even more incredible, the counselors acted like waiters, bringing chocolate milk, orange juice, and soda to the kids at each table.

"Wow, this is amazing," Brodie said, scooping a handful of M&M's onto his waffles. "My mom doesn't even let me eat this stuff at home."

"No joke," Harper replied. "We must be dreaming."

As they continued filling their plates, they saw Director McGee enter the main doors across the room. He was wearing another goofy hat, which looked like a giant banana. He approached the food line and began chatting with all the campers.

When he got to Harper and Brodie, he stuck out his hand for them to shake.

Brodie reached for it, and a shock buzzed through his hand. He quickly took it back and tried to shake out the strange tingly feeling.

Director McGee laughed and held up his palm, revealing a hand-buzzer from a gag shop.

"Gotcha!" he said, laughing at his own joke. "Boy, I'm going to miss this. How did you campers sleep last night?"

"Good, I guess," Harper answered, still annoyed by the hand-buzzer prank on Brodie. She wasn't sure what to think about Director McGee. "I admit, the built-in sound machines on each bunk and the celestial projection on the ceiling were pretty relaxing."

"Yeah, soft music was playing in our cabin all night," Brodie added. "I probably could have slept through the entire week if the counselors hadn't woken us up this morning with their barbershop quartet rendition of 'Oh, What a Beautiful Mornin''!"

Director McGee chuckled.

"I'm glad you both got plenty of rest. You're going to need it for all the fun things we have planned this week."

They watched as Director McGee continued his rounds, encouraging campers to eat to their heart's desire. He even stopped and placed a whoopee cushion in a chair and belly-laughed when he heard a camper sit on it.

A few moments later, Director McGee stepped up to the microphone on the stage at the front of the room. He cleared his throat and addressed the crowd. "Good mornin', campers! I know that your counselors informed you last night that you can write letters home to your parents, and I wanted to let you know that you can drop them off in the blue basket that we'll be coming around with here in a moment. I'll personally be mailing them out every day before lunch."

He held up the blue basket so that everyone could see it, then he started gathering letters from the campers, one table at a time.

"Are you going to write a letter home?" Brodie asked Harper.

"I probably should," Harper replied, debating whether to make contact with her parents while they were still trying to figure things out. Ever since they told her what was going on, she had distanced herself from them.

Nearby, Darla filled her plate with pancakes and covered them with syrup and chocolate chips. She looked like a kid in a candy store.

Director McGee stopped to talk to her for a moment.

"I can't wait to tell my family about camp!" she declared, setting down her plate and taking a family photo from her pocket to show him.

Director McGee smiled, blew a kazoo in her

face, and continued on to another table.

Darla kissed the photo and started to put it back in her pocket. But Regina, who had been watching her, walked by and knocked the photo out of her hand, also bumping the syrup bottle off the buffet table.

The syrup spilled onto the tile floor, drenching the family photo.

"No!" Darla cried out, reaching her hand to the floor to save the photo.

"No one cares about your stupid picture," Regina said. "If you were smart, you'd have it backed up on your Instagram."

With tears in her eyes, Darla peered down at the photo. The syrup had covered the faces of her brothers, sisters, and parents.

"Oh, wait, you probably don't have Instagram because you're not old enough to have a phone yet. I don't think they should allow kids into camp that aren't even old enough to have a phone," Regina said, jabbing a final blow, and then she walked away.

Harper hurried to Darla's side.

"It's ruined," Darla said, feeling defeated.

"Here, let me help," Harper offered, fetching a roll of paper towels and trying to wipe the syrup off the photo. But the harder she rubbed at it, the more damage she did. "You shouldn't listen to anything Regina says. I don't know what's wrong with her."

Harper hoped Darla might conjure a smile, but she seemed too sad, like the light inside her had been snuffed out.

During breakfast, Harper sat next to Darla. While they ate, Counselor Fuller conducted the morning roll call. All the while, Harper could feel Regina staring at them from the other end of the table. It was as if, for whatever reason, she had it out for Darla.

Once everyone was checked off the list, Counselor Fuller gave them instructions for the morning. "All right, ladies. It's time to match up with a buddy."

Regina and Tabitha immediately paired up. All the other girls did the same.

Harper turned to Darla. "Want to be my buddy?"

Without looking up, Darla gave a slight nod.

Counselor Fuller continued, "Unfortunately, Director McGee says it's too foggy to go to the waterpark today, so the girls will be playing bazooka ball in the gym while the boys head over to the laser tag arena. We'll switch during snack break and will have an epic indoor game of capture-the-flag this afternoon—boys against girls!"

She waved for the girls to follow her, and Harper and Darla quickly cleaned off their trays and joined the other girls.

When they arrived in the gym, there were a dozen blue and red dodgeballs lined up at the center of the court. But even more interesting were the cannon-like contraptions leaning against the walls.

"Half of you on each side!" Counselor Fuller instructed in a voice a bit more stern than her usual chipper one. "We're going to play three rounds. When the whistle blows, fetch the balls at the center of the court, and bring them back to your team's bazookas to launch at the other side. No aiming at the face—only the body. The

46

winning team gets first dibs at the chocolate buffet tonight."

Regina and Tabitha ran to the left side of the court with ten other girls. Harper and Darla joined the rest on the right side.

Everyone stood behind the white line, waiting for the whistle to blow.

Harper did her best to ignore the butterflies in her stomach. She always felt nervous before any kind of competition or performance— whether it was a spelling contest, volleyball game, or piano recital.

She noticed Darla standing off to the side next to one of the cannons and realized that Darla was feeling even more nervous than she was.

Even worse, Regina was staring daggers at Darla from across the gym.

"You want to take off your glasses and let Counselor Fuller hold them?" Harper asked.

Darla shook her head. "I can't see anything without them," she replied, more timid than usual.

"Just stay behind me, okay?" Harper said. "I'll keep an eye on Regina."

Darla nodded and hid herself behind Harper.

As soon as Counselor Fuller blew the whistle, Harper sprinted toward the center of the court while Darla stayed behind her. Close to the wall.

Regina was the first girl from either side to grab a rubber ball and make it back to her team's cannon. She loaded it quickly, then took aim and launched it across the gym as hard as she could.

Harper watched in distress as the ball spun, as if in slow motion, directly toward Darla . . .

And then it knocked off her head.

# 7

# WEIRD

**H**arper ran to where Darla's head tumbled to the gym floor. It was bloodred.

Only . . .

It wasn't Darla's head.

It was the ball. It had hit her face so hard that it had seemed like her head had popped off.

Like a twig, her glasses had snapped in two over her nose and fallen to the ground. One of the lenses burst out of the frame and cracked down the middle in the crooked shape of a lightning bolt.

Darla collapsed onto the floor.

"You jerk!" Harper yelled across the gym at Regina, then ran over to help Darla. Her little body looked lifeless as a slug.

Just then, a whistle echoed throughout the gym.

"I said no aiming at faces!" Counselor Fuller scolded Regina while hurrying to Darla's side.

Counselor Fuller and Harper helped Darla down the hall to the camp nurse, and Harper waited outside the door. She put the remnants of Darla's glasses in a plastic bag, hoping they might be able to repair them later.

*Regina is awful*, Harper thought. *She's going to keep making Darla's life miserable unless I can find a way to stop her.*

Right then, Brodie walked by. His frizzy black hair looked like it could be nesting a family of crows.

"What are you doing here?" Harper asked, surprised to see him.

"I was dropping off a letter to my parents," Brodie said, pointing to Director McGee's office at the end of the hall. "Just letting them know

I've been taking my medicine."

He noticed the sign on the door. "What are you doing outside the nurse's office?"

"I'm waiting for Darla to get out. Regina launched a dodgeball at her and broke her glasses," Harper explained, holding up the plastic bag.

Brodie sighed and shook his head, bothered by something.

"Weird," he said.

"*Weird?* It was downright cruel."

"What I mean is—" Brodie stopped himself and looked around. Then he stepped closer to Harper and whispered, "It's weird because I saw a list of all the campers on Director McGee's desk."

"Yeah. So?"

"So . . . Regina's name wasn't anywhere on it. It's like she isn't even supposed to be here."

That night in the girls' cabin, Harper helped tape Darla's glasses back together. After all, Darla still had one good lens left. Nurse Betty had told Darla to keep ice on her nose for the rest of the day, and Darla was now lying in the bottom bunk bed with her face to the wall, crying silently.

"It's okay to cry," Harper said. "But you might not want to let Regina and Tabitha see you. It will only make things worse."

What she really wanted to say was that Regina and Tabitha were like vultures circling a wounded animal, waiting for it to die.

Outside, the fog seemed to be getting thicker. And darker.

"I just want to go home," Darla whimpered. "This place isn't what I thought it would be."

Harper sighed and put her hand on Darla's shoulder. "It can only get better, right? I mean, if you act like what they say and do doesn't bother you, then they'll eventually stop. My mom told me that's how bullies work."

"But how do I *act* like it doesn't bother me?" Darla asked.

Right then, Harper heard Regina laugh from the other side of the room. It was loud, unfeeling, even cruel.

"Oh, is poor Darla homesick?" Regina mocked, then added sarcastically in a whiny baby's voice, "Does she need her mommy and daddy?"

"Be quiet, Regina!" Harper yelled, and the cabin grew quiet. "Haven't you done enough damage for one day?"

Regina walked across the cabin to Harper's and Darla's bunks. Tabitha followed after her like a loyal pet.

"I wasn't talking to you," Regina said, threatening Harper. Then she turned to Darla again. "I wouldn't go to sleep tonight if I were you. Nighttime is when ghosts possess people and take over their bodies and minds. If we hear a scream coming from the cove tonight, we should just hand you over, and the ghost girl will leave the rest of us alone. You could be like our sacrificial offering."

"Stop it," Harper demanded.

Regina glared at her. Before she could say anything back, Counselor Fuller walked into the cabin.

"Lights out! Everyone in their bunks."

Regina and Tabitha scurried back to their beds, acting innocent. Harper climbed up the ladder to the top bunk, leaving Darla sulking alone in her bed below.

A moment later, the lights flicked off.

In the darkness, before the noise machines came on, Harper could hear the sound of the ceiling fan creaking as it spun around and around. The crickets chirped and the cicadas rattled outside. And the springs of the bunks squeaked as the girls gossiped in the dark, tossing and turning in their beds.

Then . . .

Harper thought she heard Darla whispering something below.

Over and over again.

Like a chant. Or incantation.

Harper leaned over the side of the bunk so that she could hear what Darla was saying.

"I wish I could make them pay. . . . I wish I could make them pay. . . . I wish I could make them pay. . . ."

The words turned Harper's blood cold.

It seemed unlike Darla to threaten to hurt someone—even a bully.

*Every person has a breaking point,* Harper thought.

And when she glanced over the edge of her bunk, she saw something even more disturbing on Darla's face. . . .

A smile.

That looked a lot like evil.

# 8

# MISSING

When Harper entered the mess hall the next morning for breakfast, she didn't see Darla at their usual table. And when Darla's name was called out during roll call, Darla didn't answer.

"Has anyone seen the little girl with pink bows in her pigtails?" Counselor Fuller asked.

Everyone at the table shook their heads.

"How about you? Do you know anything?" Counselor Fuller asked, looking at Harper.

"Darla wasn't in her bed when I woke up this morning," Harper said. "I figured she had just gotten up early to come to breakfast."

"Hmm. Would you mind going and checking the cabin again?"

"Sure," Harper said, and headed toward the door.

On her way out, she approached Brodie, who was eating a stack of chocolate-covered waffles.

"Will you come with me?" she asked.

"Where?"

"To look for Darla. They don't know where she is."

Concerned, Brodie abandoned his waffles and followed Harper outside.

They ambled through the fog with their flashlights. Even though it was midmorning, it was still difficult to see anything. It felt like they were walking around on another planet.

"I hope Darla's okay," Brodie said, shining his beam behind a thicket of bushes.

"Me too," Harper replied. "The sooner we find her, the better."

They checked the girls' cabin. But Darla wasn't there. So they decided to continue their search before heading back to the mess hall.

"Do you think that Regina and Tabitha could have done something to her?" Brodie asked.

"I don't know," Harper admitted, having secretly been wondering the same thing. "I mean, they're terrible, for sure. But I don't know if they'd actually do anything to hurt her."

"Didn't they launch a bazooka ball at her face?"

Harper realized Brodie was right. Regina and Tabitha had already proven that they had it in them to hurt Darla physically.

"I did hear Darla say last night in the cabin that she didn't like camp and wanted to go home," Harper said. "Maybe she snuck away while everyone was sleeping."

"You mean, like, hitchhike home in the middle of the night?"

"Maybe," Harper said.

"Surely she'd know better than to do something like that," Brodie replied. "If I've learned anything from movies, it's that there are a lot scarier people out there in the world than Regina and Tabitha."

"She didn't seem herself last night," Harper said.

She paused, pondering over a thought that had been tucked in the back of her head.

"What is it?" Brodie asked, sensing she was distracted.

"It's just that . . . the last thing I heard Darla say before bed was that she wanted to make Regina and Tabitha 'pay.' I didn't know what she meant, but do you think she could have run off to hide in the woods to play a prank on Regina and Tabitha? You know, like, make them feel bad for bullying her?"

"That'd be way twisted," Brodie replied.

"Yeah," Harper agreed. "She's too inno-cent—she couldn't have thought up anything that manipulative. At least I don't think she would have. I mean, it's not like we know her that well."

They walked farther down the path, search-ing every inch of ground.

Rocks.

Grass.

Mud.

Twigs.

Pine needles.

But still no sign of Darla.

As they passed by the yellow caution tape at the ladder to the zip-line platform, Brodie stopped to look around.

Then . . .

His eyes grew wide, and Harper followed his gaze to the gray water washing up against the bank.

Brodie shined his flashlight at the ground, and his jaw dropped.

Harper's did too.

Together, they stared down at the ominous scene.

"Shoe prints," Harper whispered. "They're in the mud leading up to the bank."

"And straight into the water," Brodie added.

Even creepier . . .

There, at the edge of the cove, were Darla's broken glasses.

Covered in a fluorescent green slime.

# 9

# NO EVIDENCE

Harper and Brodie ran as fast as they could back to the mess hall. The cool mist filled their lungs and stung their faces.

When they arrived at the main office, they found Counselor Fuller and Director McGee looking over what Harper assumed was the camper list.

When Director McGee saw Harper and Brodie, he hid the list behind his back.

"You both have to come quick!" Harper shouted. "We found Darla's glasses and shoe prints by the cove!"

"What?" Director McGee said. "I think you must be mistaken."

"We have to hurry!" Brodie urged.

"Calm down," Counselor Fuller chimed in. "There's no need to worry yourselves. I've already spoken with Director McGee. Nurse Betty sent Darla home early this morning with a severe stomachache. It seems she ate too much popcorn, candy, and soda at the movie last night."

Harper and Brodie exchanged a confused look.

"That doesn't make any sense—she didn't seem sick," Harper said. "Can you please just come look at what we found? There's something really weird by the cove."

"Yeah, you have to see it," Brodie added.

Director McGee stuffed the camper list into a drawer and locked it. Then he and Counselor Fuller grabbed their flashlights and followed Harper and Brodie out the door.

When Director McGee and Counselor Fuller noticed the lock on the nearby canoe shack had been broken and the door was open, they grew more concerned.

"If someone went into the cove, I hope they were wearing a life vest," Director McGee worried aloud as they hurried down the dirt path.

"It would be difficult to find their way back in the fog," Counselor Fuller added nervously.

Harper sensed that they were both uneasy.

"So the story about the girl who drowned . . . did that really happen, or did you guys just make that up?" Harper asked.

Director McGee and Counselor Fuller didn't reply.

When they arrived at the cove, Brodie led them straight to the site. He shined his flashlight around on the bank. But there was nothing there.

No shoe prints.

No glasses.

No slime.

"It was right here, wasn't it?" Brodie asked Harper.

"Yeah. The shoe prints led to that spot right

there," she said, shining her flashlight beam in the very place where the glasses and prints had been.

But the mud on the bank looked untouched. And it was covered in moss.

"Maybe you two just thought you saw something in the fog," Director McGee said.

"The good news is that Darla's home safe and sound, and no other campers are in danger," Counselor Fuller added. "I'll check around about the canoe shack—I'm sure one of the counselors just forgot to lock it up."

Brodie shook his head in disbelief. "I know what I saw."

"Yeah, the slime was right there," Harper said.

"Did you say slime?" Director McGee asked. "We have buckets of it stored in the activities closet for Slime Night later in the week. Someone must have gotten into it."

Harper and Brodie looked at each other, feeling silly for possibly making a big deal out of nothing.

"Why don't you two come back to the mess hall? Clear your minds for a bit," Director McGee said.

Harper and Brodie both peered out to the cove, wondering what was out there.

But there was only silence.

And fog.

That night, as Harper lay in her bunk staring at the ceiling, she couldn't help but wonder if Darla really was back at home with her family. She wished she had some way to check on her, but she knew the reality was that she'd probably never see or talk to Darla again.

Harper's thoughts were soon interrupted by Regina's voice across the cabin. . . .

"I'm glad that girl is finally gone," Regina said to Tabitha. "I was so tired of listening to her talk about her family this and her family that."

Harper sat up in her bed.

"You don't stop, do you?" Harper said.

Regina glared at her.

"She was annoying," Regina replied. "Her parents probably just got rid of her for the week because they didn't want her in the house all summer. And now they're probably mad that she got sick at the beginning of camp and ruined their free time. She shouldn't even have been here in the first place."

"How can you be so insensitive?" Harper asked. "Besides, Brodie saw the camper list, and your name isn't even on it. If anyone's not supposed to be here, it's you."

At Harper's accusation, Regina stood from her bed and walked over to her.

"I have more of a right to be here than any-one!" Regina shouted, jabbing her finger into Harper's chest. "You better be careful, Harper. Wouldn't want anything bad to happen to you too."

With a sinister smirk on her face, Regina walked back to her bunk.

*She has the same look that Darla had last night*, Harper thought. *Evil.*

A few minutes later, Counselor Fuller came

in and turned out the lights and activated the sound machines.

Harper lay on her back again looking at the ceiling in the dark. She couldn't shake the heavy feeling in her gut. It kept prodding her, taunting her, warning her. *There's something wrong with Camp Moon Lake.*

And she was right.

There was something wrong indeed.

Something very, very wrong.

# 10

# VANISHED

**H**arper awoke in the night.

The cabin was dark and quiet, and she could hear the breeze whispering through the pine trees outside.

She sat up in bed and looked around.

Everyone was asleep. And everything seemed normal. She figured a spider or bug had crawled across her face while she was sleeping and woken her up.

And she was just about to lie back down when she saw . . .

Two silhouettes. On the far side of the cabin. Sneaking out the screen door.

*Regina and Tabitha,* she thought, noticing their beds were empty. *Where are they going in the middle of the night?*

Harper grabbed her flashlight and climbed down the ladder of her bunk. She tiptoed across the cabin, careful not to awaken the other campers. Then she crept out the door.

The fog wrapped around her like a blanket, tickling her face with its cool wetness. It was so thick, she couldn't tell which direction the girls had gone.

But she soon heard laughter. And followed after it.

The dirt felt cool against her bare feet, and for a moment, she wondered if she might be dreaming.

Every time she thought she had lost Regina and Tabitha, she heard their laughter again coming from a different direction.

*What are they doing?* she wondered. *Maybe I should go back to the cabin where it's safe. I can ask them about it in the morning.*

But her curiosity got the best of her.

After a while, she no longer heard their

voices or saw their footprints in the dirt. And she no longer knew where she was.

She was all alone.

In the dark.

Where no one could hear her if she cried for help.

Just then . . .

Someone screamed.

A bloodcurdling, desperate shriek—a sound she never wanted to hear again.

Harper hesitated for a moment, then ran toward it.

An awful feeling ate at her stomach.

That's when her flashlight beam illumined the yellow caution tape of the zip-line ladder five feet in front of her.

*Something terrible has happened to Regina and Tabitha*, she thought, unable to locate their footprints or any sign of them near the ladder. *I have to find a place to hide.*

She ran in the direction of the nearby canoe shack and climbed through an unlocked window. Out of breath, she lay down in a dusty nook where she doubted anyone could find her.

*I'll hide here until morning*, she thought.

But her eyes soon became heavy, and she slipped away into a dreamless sleep.

A rooster's crow woke her up just after dawn.

She sat up and brushed the dirt out of her hair. When she glanced out the window, she saw the fog wrapping its smoky fingers around the trees. It looked alive.

Harper rose to her feet, then rushed out of the canoe shack and toward the mess hall.

*They're probably all worried about where I am*, she thought.

But when she entered through the doors, all the campers and counselors were at their tables, finishing up breakfast. Like they didn't even know she was missing.

"What are you doing here?" Brodie said, surprised to see Harper. "I thought you went home."

"What?" she asked. "Why would you think that?"

"You didn't answer during roll call, and Director McGee said you, Regina, and Tabitha had been sent home with a stomach bug in the middle of the night."

Harper squinted, confused.

"Why would they say that? I saw Regina and Tabitha sneak out of the cabin last night, and I followed them. But I lost them near the zip line. I don't know what happened to them, but they definitely weren't sick."

Brodie looked around, suspicious.

"Weird," he said.

Just then, Harper saw Director McGee and Counselor Fuller standing off to the side talking to a group of counselors. Harper rushed toward them. Brodie followed.

"Why did you tell the other campers that I was sent home?" Harper asked, pulling on Director McGee's sleeve.

At the sight of her, Director McGee's eyes grew wide. Counselor Fuller's grew even wider.

"Harper? What are you doing here? I—I thought you went home," Counselor Fuller said, seemingly just as confused as Harper.

"Why would you think that?"

"That's what Nurse Betty's report said this morning after we did the roll call. She said you, Regina, and Tabitha stopped by her office sometime after midnight with a stomach bug, and that she called the bus driver to take you all home."

Harper couldn't believe what she was hearing. Someone had completely made up a story about her.

"Well, it's not true. I saw Regina and Tabitha sneak out of the cabin last night, and I followed them to see what they were up to. I lost them in the fog near the zip line, right after I heard one of them scream."

Director McGee and Counselor Fuller exchanged a worried look.

"Maybe Nurse Betty got confused—she does that sometimes," Director McGee said, then turned to Counselor Fuller. "I'll check in with her. You go find the bus driver."

Counselor Fuller nodded, and they both disappeared out the nearby door.

But ten minutes later, they returned to the

mess hall with a panicked look in their eyes.

"Did you talk to them? What did they say?" Harper asked, eager to find out the news.

"They're both gone," Director McGee said, seeming exasperated and perplexed. "When I approached them and told them that you were still here at camp, they ran onto the bus and drove away. It's obvious they're up to something—hopefully not as terrible as it seems. I've called the police, and I need to inform the rest of the campers about what's going on."

"If Nurse Betty lied about me, Regina, and Tabitha, then that means she probably lied about Darla too."

"It's possible," Director McGee said solemnly. "But we don't have any time to waste trying to chase down Nurse Betty and the bus driver. We'll leave that to the police. For now, we need to focus on keeping all the campers safe."

He hurried to the stage and turned on the microphone. A piercing sound rang through the speakers.

He wiped the sweat from his forehead and addressed the crowd. . . .

"Kids, I—I have something urgent I need to share with you. It seems that several campers have gone missing. We're not certain of the situation yet, but the police are contacting your parents right now to inform them about what's going on and request that they come pick you up immediately. Because of our policy of secrecy, there's no internet and only one phone line here at camp, and we need to leave it open in case the police call. So you won't be able to call your parents directly."

"What about our cell phones?" a boy at the front asked.

A few other campers grunted in agreement.

"There aren't any cell towers this far into the woods, so trying would be no use."

Harper gulped. "This is serious," she said, hardly believing what she was hearing.

"No joke," Brodie replied.

Then Counselor Fuller walked onto the stage and whispered something in Director McGee's ear.

His eyes widened. With a quaver in his voice, he continued, "W-we've decided it's best to go into lockdown mode. In a few moments, we're going to send you all to your cabins with a buddy and ask that you bring your stuff back here to the mess hall. Once everyone is inside, we're going to lock the doors until we can figure out what's going on and your parents arrive. We have lots of activities we can do inside. And plenty of food. So everyone will be okay here."

Harper watched as Director McGee hurried off the stage and disappeared into the hallway. The remaining counselors walked around to the tables recapping the plan to the campers.

*I'm not staying here for another minute,* Harper thought. *I'm going home.*

But what she didn't know was that she would never go home again.

# 11

# NOT THE FIRST TIME

"This is crazy," Harper said as she and Brodie cleaned off their trays and stacked them on the conveyor belt that transported them back into the kitchen. "Kids are disappearing from camp, and the counselors want us to sit around and pretend like everything's okay. Surely they have other buses they can call to come get us!"

Brodie glanced around the room.

Everyone was panicked. Some kids were crying. Others sat pale with fright.

"Director McGee said our parents should be on the way," he replied. "Besides, do you have a better idea?"

"Yeah. The counselors are all distracted right now," Harper said. "I say we go find the phone."

"I'm staying right here like they said," Brodie replied. "It's the safest option."

"Suit yourself," she said, then snuck around the corner and out the door.

Harper glanced over her shoulder at Brodie, hoping he might change his mind. But instead he gave her a reluctant wave of good luck.

Then she let the door close behind her.

On her way down the dimly lit hallway, she wished more than anything she could talk to her mom and dad. Even if things were rough between them, the wall she had put up now seemed so petty in the face of her current situation.

*I bet they've made their decision by now*, she thought. *I wish things could just go back to the way they were.*

Harper rounded the corner at the end of the hall, hurried into the main office, and reached for the phone.

But someone else's hand grabbed it first.

"What are you doing in here, young lady?" Director McGee asked in a more serious voice than the one he usually used. He had been sitting in a tall leather chair with his back to her, so she hadn't seen him.

"I'm—I'm calling my parents to make sure they're on their way," Harper explained.

"I already told you—all parents are currently being notified by the police. We need to leave this line open for the time being."

"What about the cell phones—can't I just try to use mine real quick? You can even sit here and watch me to make sure I don't take any photos with it or whatever," Harper said, noticing the locked box of cell phones behind the desk.

Director McGee shook his head.

"Camp policy. Besides, like I told the campers, even if I did give yours back to you, there are no cell towers this far into the woods," Director McGee replied. "Don't worry—we have everything under control. You just have to trust us."

"But everything's not under control," Harper

said. "Kids are going missing, and you don't know where they are!"

Director McGee sighed. He calmly reached into a drawer and took out two sheets of blank paper, a pen, and an envelope.

He held them out to Harper.

"I understand you're scared. Like I said earlier, why don't you take some time and write out your thoughts and fears in a letter?"

"But I thought you said all the parents were being told to come pick us up today. So why would I need to write a letter?"

"Because it will make you feel better," Director McGee said, encouraging her. "I'll overnight it so that they get it first thing tomorrow morning—if they aren't already here by then."

Harper glanced at the landline phone again, wishing she could just make the phone call. Something in her didn't trust Director McGee.

"Fine," she surrendered, half wishing she hadn't given in so easily.

She took the pen, paper, and envelope, walked out of the office, down the hall, and to a chair in a corner next to a window.

As she sat down, the fog stretched right up to the pane and curled around the building, like it was wrapping its claws around them.

Anxious, Harper looked down at the blank page, then took up her pen and wrote the following message to her parents:

*Dear Mom and Dad,*
*Please come get me right away. Kids are disappearing from camp. Something's not right about this place.*
*—Harper*

*PS I love you both.*
*We can talk more when you pick me up, but I'll be okay wherever I have to live—even if it means going back and forth between two houses.*

She set down the pen and immediately felt a heavy weight lift from her shoulders. Writing down her thoughts and feelings had somehow

made her feel a little better. She had said everything she wanted to say in only a few sentences.
And she now felt some hope.

Harper folded the letter and sealed it in the
envelope. The gross taste of the sealant lingered
on her tongue. Then she walked back down the
hall to Director McGee's office.

He was still sitting at his desk, staring into
thin air, as if he wasn't sure what to do next.
Harper could tell that he felt overwhelmed with
emotions and responsibilities.

She handed the letter to him.

"Thank you, Harper. I'm sure your parents
will be here soon since your town is only a few
hours away, but like I said, I'll overnight this
just in case." He paused, then added, "And I'm
really sorry camp hasn't turned out the way you
hoped. It's not usually like this. And this isn't
how we ever wanted it to be."

Harper had always been good at reading
people, and she could tell Director McGee felt
genuinely sorry.

"It's not your fault, I guess. But you might

want to change your brochures for next summer," Harper said, half joking. Director McGee cracked a smile. Then Harper added, "And it's up to you to figure out what's going on soon. Before anything else bad happens."

"The lockdown should prevent any other incidents from taking place," Director McGee said. "You better go get with a buddy and head to your cabin to gather all your stuff. Once everyone's inside the mess hall, we'll lock the doors."

Harper nodded, then headed back toward the hallway. But when she looked over her shoulder, she noticed something in Director McGee's eyes. Something secret. And it gave her the feeling this wasn't the first time kids had gone missing from Camp Moon Lake.

# 12

# FOG LIGHTS

As she walked down the hall, Harper couldn't stop thinking about the unsettling look in Director McGee's eyes. She was sure he knew something he wasn't telling them. After all, his family had run the camp for five generations, so if anyone knew what might be going on, it was him.

*Maybe I'm just paranoid*, she thought. *There might be a logical explanation for all of this.*

As if she wasn't suspicious enough, she was suddenly overcome by the feeling that she was being watched.

The hairs on the back of her neck stood up. Her body tensed.

She slowly turned and saw a tall, thin figure standing ten feet behind her in the dark.

Before she could turn on her flashlight, the figure spoke.

"Harper, it's me," Brodie said, walking out of the shadows.

She sighed in relief, then nudged his arm as he approached.

"You can't sneak up on me like that," Harper said.

"Sorry," Brodie replied. "I decided I couldn't leave you on your own. I was just going to see if you wanted me to walk with you to your cabin to get your stuff. I already grabbed mine."

"Sure," Harper said, comforted by the idea of walking with a friend.

They headed out the main doors and into the misty world beyond the mess hall. Even with their flashlights, they could see only five feet in front of them. The fog was twice as thick as it had been the day before. It seemed to be getting denser every hour.

"I guess we were wrong about Regina and Tabitha," Harper said. "But I've been thinking. If the story about the ghost girl is true, then what if she really is possessing kids at the camp?"

"Or maybe you're just imagining things," Brodie replied. "I heard Counselor Fuller talking to another counselor. It sounds like Regina might not be as bad as we thought. Apparently, she's been having a hard time at home."

"What do you mean?"

"Her parents are splitting up," Brodie revealed. "And they sent her to camp last minute while they try to figure out who she's going to live with after the divorce."

Harper was stunned. She and Regina were both going through something similar.

A series of images reeled through Harper's mind. . . .

Darla talking about her own family just before Regina broke the trust fall. . . .

Darla being proud of her family photo

moments before Regina ruined it with the syrup. . . .

Darla talking about wanting to go home to her family on the night before she disappeared. . . .

Harper soon realized that every time Regina had bullied Darla, it was after Darla said something positive about her own family.

Deep down, Harper felt sorry for Regina.

When Harper and Brodie arrived at the girls' cabin a few moments later, Harper crept inside and grabbed her sleeping bag and suitcase. Before leaving, she glanced at Darla's bunk and then at Regina's and Tabitha's. Their stuff was all still there, just as they had left it.

But she noticed something else on Regina's bunk.

Something green.

And wet.

Harper walked closer to get a better look. She reached down and touched the strange substance.

"Slime," she whispered, observing the

glowing goo on her fingertips. It looked radioactive, even otherworldly.

She hurried outside to show Brodie. He examined the ooze, then said, "This is the same stuff we saw on Darla's glasses by the cove. It's as green as Slimer from *Ghostbusters*."

"Do you think this could all just be part of an elaborate hoax?" Harper asked. "Director McGee did say he was going to be playing twice as many pranks since this is his retirement week."

Brodie glared down at the green goo, then shook his head. "There's no way this is the same gag slime that Director McGee said we're using on Slime Night. This looks like it belongs in a high-security laboratory."

They stared at it for another moment, then Brodie finally said, "Come on. Let's get out of here."

He took Harper's sleeping bag and suitcase and carried them under his arms.

As they hurried back up the path to the mess hall, Harper couldn't shake the feeling that they were being watched. This time for real.

"Is it me or is someone following us?" she asked.

Brodie stopped and turned in a full circle with his flashlight.

"I don't hear or see anything. What made you say that?"

"It's just a feeling. Down in my gut," she admitted.

Just then, an unnatural sound emanated from the direction of the cove. It sounded like bats or birds screeching in a horror movie. Then it grew into a low moan, like something from another dimension.

Harper turned toward the cove and saw something she couldn't explain. . . .

Two beams of light glowed in the fog.

Bright as spotlights.

And they were hovering over the water, mid-air.

"W-what's that?" Harper whispered.

"I don't know," Brodie said, his eyes wide in fright.

"Just then, the light beams floated across the cove and disappeared into the unknown.

"W-were those, like, super-strong flashlights or something?" Harper asked, a tremor in her voice.

"I—I don't think so," Brodie replied.

"What were they, then?"

Brodie gulped. "You'll think I'm crazy, but they looked like something's . . . eyes."

# 13

# HAUNTED

They sprinted toward the mess hall as fast as they could.

Once inside, they saw the counselors setting up tables and filling them with cakes, pies, brownies, ice cream, and sodas. It was a junk food wonderland.

They spotted Counselor Fuller pacing back and forth in front of the stage, and they hurried over to her.

"Counselor Fuller, we saw something hovering over the water in the cove," Harper said, out of breath.

Counselor Fuller stopped pacing and glared down at Harper.

"What are you talking about?" she asked. "What did you see?"

"I don't know exactly," Harper replied. "But it didn't look like anything I've ever seen before."

"I saw it too," Brodie affirmed. "It had these crazy light-beam eyes. They were glowing like—like spotlights!"

"Do you think it's the ghost girl? Or—or maybe Nurse Betty and the bus driver kidnapping and hiding the campers somewhere?" Harper asked.

"It's not that simple," Counselor Fuller admitted. She sat down in a chair. "Nurse Betty and the bus driver ran away because they know it's their fault that campers are going missing. But they're not the ones taking them."

"Huh?" Harper squinted in confusion.

Counselor Fuller pondered something for a moment, then stood and pulled Harper and Brodie off to the side.

She took a deep breath. "What have you two

heard about Camp Moon Lake?"

"What do you mean?" Harper replied. "Just that it's the most magical summer camp on earth."

"Besides that. I mean, have you heard any weird rumors or strange stories?" Counselor Fuller clarified.

Brodie's ears perked at the prospect of creepy camp stories.

"Just the one about the girl who drowned," Harper said. "Did it really happen?"

Counselor Fuller pursed her lips, as if debating whether to tell them something she wasn't supposed to tell.

"We're not allowed to talk about it for liability reasons, but you two have seen too much already." She paused, then whispered, "Camp Moon Lake is . . . haunted. And not just by the ghost girl."

This time, Harper wished that Counselor Fuller was trying to play a prank on them. But she had the feeling what Counselor Fuller was saying was no joke.

"Haunted? Like with ghosts?" Harper asked.

Counselor Fuller nodded. "You see, a long, long time ago, Camp Moon Lake was unknowingly built on top of an ancient burial ground," she revealed. "We've tried to cover it up with fancy buildings and such, but some things just won't stay buried."

"Oh, man," Brodie said with morbid delight. "You're telling me we're standing on top of a graveyard right now? A real graveyard with dead people right beneath our feet?"

"Unfortunately, yes," Counselor Fuller replied. "Usually, the spirits leave us alone if we leave them alone. But Nurse Betty and the bus driver accidentally disturbed the graves last week, and it's been causing problems to say the least. Director McGee got on to them about it when he found out and decided to go ahead and have camp anyway since it's his last week."

Harper couldn't believe what she was hearing. It felt like a nightmare had seeped out of her head and was coming to life in the real world.

And she now understood Director McGee was acting so weird because he felt guilty for green-lighting camp even though he had known there was a risk.

"Now that's what I call a twist," Brodie whispered.

"Is that what's causing the fog? The ghosts?" Harper asked, surprised that Counselor Fuller was trusting them with such a big secret.

Counselor Fuller nodded and continued, "Whenever there have been hauntings in the past, the fog has always been present. The best thing we can do is stay inside away from it. Once the fog goes away, everything should be fine again."

"But what about the kids it's already taken? Will the ghosts give them back?" Harper asked.

"I don't know," Counselor Fuller answered. "But you two need to stick together."

Harper felt goose bumps prickle her skin. She looked out at all the kids gorging themselves with cupcakes and cookies, completely unaware of the truth.

Before Harper could ask another question, Counselor Fuller scurried off to talk to another counselor.

With no other choice in sight, she and Brodie dragged their sleeping bags over to the corner of the mess hall and sat down.

They were both silent for a few moments, then Harper asked, "Is this really happening?"

"I don't know. Maybe we're asleep, and this is all just a bad dream. You want me to make up a story to keep your mind off things?" Brodie offered.

"No thanks. We're living inside a story right now—a scary one!" she replied.

Brodie put his hand on her shoulder, and Harper noticed Counselor Fuller watching them from across the room.

"Don't worry, Harper. Everything's going to turn out fine," Brodie assured her. "You'll see. Real life doesn't have twist endings."

But by the next night, Harper would think otherwise.

# 14

## CONTACT

By lunchtime that day, six campers still hadn't made it back from their cabins with their luggage. Director McGee said he suspected the kids had gotten lost in the fog, but based on what Counselor Fuller had told her, Harper suspected that wasn't the whole truth.

Director McGee had sent out a group of counselors to go look for them, but they returned with no success.

The remaining campers spent the day in the mess hall, trying to suppress their worries with junk food. As soon as one tray of cupcakes or cookies was gone, another one was brought out from the kitchen. It was an endless feast of sweets. Harper figured that every camper was going to be ten pounds heavier by the time their parents came to pick them up.

She, on the other hand, couldn't work up an appetite.

All day long, she waited for her parents to arrive, but they never came.

It was the same all night and the next day as well.

She waited . . . and waited.

But they never showed up.

By sunset of that next day, with no rescue in sight, Harper decided to take matters into her own hands.

While all the other campers were rolling out their sleeping bags in the main room to camp out for another night, she approached Brodie. He was sitting on the floor, writing a story about the camp vanishings.

"Don't you think it's weird that no police or parents have shown up yet?" Harper asked. "I mean, kids have gone missing. That's sort of a big deal. If our parents really were notified, then why aren't they here yet?"

"Yeah, it is kind of weird," Brodie said, fully focused on his story. "But Counselor Fuller told us things should be fine once the fog goes away."

"So we're supposed to just stick around for another night and hope our parents come tomorrow?" she asked.

"What other choice do we have?" Brodie replied.

Harper glanced across the room at Director McGee, who was playing a game of cards with several other counselors. He didn't look as concerned as Harper thought he should be. In fact, he didn't seem concerned at all. Counselor Fuller, on the other hand, seemed pale with worry.

"Follow me," Harper told Brodie.

"Where are we going?" he asked, shoving his pen and notebook into his backpack.

"Just stay close," Harper instructed, then led him into the hallway.

They crept quietly, so as not to draw any attention to themselves. Their steps were soft as snowflakes, and Harper could hear the rickety sound of the air conditioner humming above. When they turned the corner at the end of the hall, she peeked into Director McGee's office.

She breathed a sigh of relief when she saw that no one was there. Then she hurried to the phone on the desk and picked it up.

"There's a dial tone!" she said.

Anxiously, Harper pressed in her mom's cell phone number, and the line began to ring.

One ring.

Two rings.

Then, on the third ring, her mom answered. "Hello?

At the sound of her mom's voice, Harper felt a surge of relief. All her worries began to fade away as she realized she could finally tell her mom everything.

"Mom, it's me!" Harper said.

"Harper? Is everything okay, sweetie?" her mom replied.

"Mom, this camp is—"

But before Harper could finish, there was a clicking sound, and the phone went silent.

No dial tone.

No voice on the other end.

Nothing.

"It—it disconnected," Harper said. She quickly unplugged the phone line and plugged it back in. But nothing happened.

Brodie reached for the computer and tried to turn it on, but the screen remained black.

Then . . .

The lights in the hall went out.

And the air conditioner stopped humming.

"The electricity's been shut off," Brodie said, noticing the fog rushing up against the window like a predator stalking its prey. "And why does it feel like whatever's out there is trying to get inside?"

Harper began pacing back and forth, trying to figure out what to do next.

"If my letter was mailed out yesterday, then my parents should have gotten it this morning, right?" she mused aloud, trying to reconvince herself. She chewed on her nails like a rabbit chomping on a carrot, which she always did when she was nervous or afraid. "Surely between my letter and the disconnected phone call, my mom and dad should be on their way right now to come get me. It kind of sounded like my mom was driving in her car when she picked up the phone. Don't you think?"

But Brodie remained silent. He was staring at something beneath Director McGee's desk.

He pointed, and Harper peeked around the corner of the desk to see what he was looking at.

All hope deflated from her.

There, in the shadows, was . . .

The blue basket.

Full of unsent letters.

# 15

# NO ESCAPE

"**W**hy weren't these mailed out?" Harper asked, noticing the envelope addressed to her parents was on the top of the pile.

"Maybe with everything going on, Director McGee forgot to send them," Brodie said.

"He forgot every day this week?" Harper asked. "Look, here's the letter you turned in to him two days ago."

Brodie was silent. There was no doubt that Director McGee had intentionally failed to mail the letters. But why?

Harper sat down in a chair next to the

bookshelf and put her face in her hands. She tried her best not to cry.

"My mom and dad aren't coming. No parents are coming," she said. "They probably don't even know what's happening here. We're on our own."

Her body felt tense. Like a storm cloud about to burst.

Then she noticed something sitting on the edge of the desk beneath a paperweight.

A stack of old photos. Some were in black and white, and others were in color but faded.

She reached for them and read the words on the back of the first photo:

*Bronson McGee Sr.*
*First Day as Director of Camp Moon Lake*

"Brodie, this is a picture of Director McGee's great-great-grandfather," she said, pointing to it. "It looks like it was taken a hundred years ago."

Brodie blinked in surprise. "He looks just like Director McGee does now. And even back then, all the other counselors are smiling that same plastic smile."

Harper turned to a photo of Bronson McGee Jr., then to one of Bronson McGee III, and even to one of Bronson McGee IV.

"Weird," Harper said. "They all look exactly alike. It's like they're clones or something."

She accidentally dropped one of the photos, and Brodie picked it up off the floor.

"Uh, Harper?" he said in a concerned voice.

"What?" she replied, not believing things could get any worse.

"Look at this," he said, holding out the photo.

Only, it wasn't a photo. It was a handwritten note from a century before.

It read:

*The secret must be kept at all costs.*

Harper felt a shiver run up her spine.

"Do you think it's talking about the camp being built on top of a graveyard?" Brodie asked.

"I don't know. But Director McGee has been lying to us the whole time."

Harper suddenly felt cold. She could feel her chest rising and falling as her breath quickened in her lungs.

"We have to get out of here," she said. "Like, *now*."

"But the mist—what if it hurts us?" Brodie asked.

"We have to take our chances. It's better than staying inside waiting for help that's never going to come," Harper replied. "We have to take care of ourselves."

Brodie handed her a flashlight. "We can take the road the bus came in on," he said. "I remember seeing a town a few miles back, just before the bus entered the fog. We can call for help there."

Harper and Brodie knew all the doors in the mess hall were locked, so they unhitched the window in Director McGee's office and climbed out into the dark, foggy night.

Once outside, Harper felt more vulnerable than ever. Like she was even closer to danger. But she knew deep down she had to take more risks before she could get to safety.

The fog felt colder, wetter, thicker than ever before.

It seemed . . .

Alive.

Harper was sure it was reading their thoughts, gauging their every move, even laughing at their plot to escape.

*I'll beat it*, she thought. *Whatever the fog is, I'll beat it.*

They managed to get away without being seen and found the road that led away from camp.

Harper and Brodie hiked in the dark for what seemed like hours. With every step they took away from camp, Harper felt safer. And less afraid.

"We should be getting close," Brodie said, taking a puff from his inhaler and squirting nose spray into his nostrils. He then reached into his backpack and handed a Twinkie to Harper.

She was just about to take it when she saw

small circular shapes of light glowing ahead in the fog.

"House lights," she said. "It's a neighborhood!"

She and Brodie ran as fast as they could, relieved to have found civilization. Harper began to smile for the first time in days.

They were moments away from safety.

From comfort.

From calling their parents!

Propelled by hope, Harper felt herself running faster than she ever had before.

She hurried onto the first porch she came upon. Brodie stayed close at her side.

Her heart chugged in her chest like a runaway train. She raised her hand to ring the doorbell, anxious to make contact with another human being.

But . . .

There was a small sign where the doorbell should have been.

The sign looked out of place.

And familiar.

*No*, she thought, squinting in the fog. *This isn't possible.*

She moved closer to the sign and read the words again:

## WELCOME TO THE GIRLS' CABIN. ENJOY YOUR STAY AT CAMP MOON LAKE!

# 16

# VANISHED

"This is impossible," Harper whispered, her stomach swirling with terror. "We were hiking away from camp the whole time. For hours!"

She spun in a circle on the cabin porch, examining her surroundings to make sure her eyes weren't playing tricks on her. Deep down, she sensed the truth, but she desperately wanted to find some clue or sign to convince her otherwise.

"It's the fog," Brodie said. "It won't let us leave."

Harper suspected he was right. They could run for days and weeks, and they'd still end up back at Camp Moon Lake.

But why?

Just then, Harper heard a terrible shriek coming from the direction of the cove.

It was the same otherworldly shrill she had heard once before, just before she saw the flashlight eyes hovering over the water.

"We have to get to a safe place," Brodie urged.

Together, they ran as fast as they could to the mess hall. Harper pushed away her fear, hiding it deep in her gut, knowing it wouldn't do her any good.

When they arrived, Harper and Brodie pounded on the locked doors and yelled for help.

But no one answered.

"Maybe they're playing games in the gym," Brodie proposed.

Harper pulled on one of the doors and was surprised to find that it was unlocked.

"That's strange," she said. "They should still be in lockdown."

She and Brodie crept through the corridor and into the main hall.

Their jaws dropped. Neither said a word.

The sight before them was unexplainable.

The entire room . . .

Was full of fog.

Invaded.

Haunted.

Seized.

The sleeping bags were still laid out on the floor.

But all of the campers . . .

And the counselors . . .

Were gone.

Vanished!

"Where did everyone go?" Harper asked, her voice trembling.

"Maybe the police finally came and rescued everyone," Brodie said. "I told you we should have stayed put."

Harper shook her head. "If that's true, then

why didn't everyone take their stuff with them?"

There was silence for a moment while they pondered the mystery.

"Look," Brodie said, pointing toward the ceiling. "If the lights are back on, that means the generators have kicked in. And if there's power, then that means—"

"The phone should be working again!" Harper finished.

They sprinted down the hall back to Director McGee's office and hurried inside. Harper gasped when she saw that the window was still open.

"We forgot to close it!" she said. "It's our fault that the fog got inside."

Brodie glanced around, searching for a more logical explanation. But there didn't seem to be one.

Just as Harper was about to pick up the phone, she noticed something about the photos on the desk. Not only did all the Bronson McGees look alike, but . . .

"Hey, did you see this?" Harper asked

Brodie. "All the Bronson McGees in these photos have the same mole in the middle of their
forehead."

Brodie's eyes grew wide.

And that's when Harper realized they didn't
just look like the same person. They *were* the
same person.

"He—he must be a vampire—or—or a—"
Brodie began in astonishment.

But before he could finish, they heard voices
coming from the room across the hall.

Quickly, Harper and Brodie hid behind
the office door and peeked around the corner.
Unsure if they could trust whoever it was, they
remained still as statues.

That's when they saw them. The faces
behind the voices.

And they weren't strangers.

Or monsters.

Or ghouls.

They were . . .

Director McGee and Counselor Fuller.

The two of them were standing in front

of a crackling fireplace in the room across the hall. Their shadows projected on the wall behind them like conspiring demons. They were whispering in a language Harper couldn't understand.

Even more chilling, as the two counselors talked, Director McGee did something Harper couldn't explain.

He reached into the flames with his bare hands and moved a simmering log to stoke the fire.

But when the flames licked his flesh, he didn't flinch. He didn't scream. And his skin didn't burn.

And that's when he and Counselor Fuller both did something else Harper had never seen anyone do before.

They began to hover . . . an entire foot off the ground.

*How did I not see it?* Harper thought. *Director McGee and Counselor Fuller are ghosts!*

# 17

# TUG-OF-WAR

**H**arper and Brodie remained behind the door in Director McGee's office, eavesdropping on the conversation across the hall.

"There's still at least one left," they heard Counselor Fuller say, now speaking a language they could understand. "The rest have been prepared."

"It's going to be a long trip to the next world," Director McGee added. "It's important that we never leave any behind. Every one of them must go."

*Long trip? Are they kidnapping campers*

*and taking them into the ghost world?* Harper wondered. *They probably didn't want us taking photos because their images wouldn't show up and they'd be caught!*

"The story I made up about the drowned girl only keeps them away from the cove for so long, so we need to move fast," Director McGee said. "And no more mistakes. The shoe prints and glasses that were left at the cove could have spoiled everything. It's important to remember our motto at all times: 'No trace left behind.'"

Harper couldn't believe what she was hearing. Nothing was making any sense.

Not wanting to stick around any longer, she motioned toward the open window. Brodie nodded in understanding, and the two of them started across the room. But as they passed the desk, Brodie accidentally knocked over a pile of books.

They made a loud clattering sound against the floor.

Director McGee and Counselor Fuller stirred in the next room.

Harper leaped toward the window and climbed out. She reached back to help Brodie, but just as his fingers touched hers, she saw two large hands grip his shoulders.

"No!" Harper shouted at Director McGee. "Let him go!"

She tugged on Brodie's arm, but Director McGee pulled harder.

"There's no use in trying to escape," Director McGee threatened, pulling Brodie back into the room. "You've been chosen for a higher purpose. You've all been chosen."

"What are you talking about? Give me back my friend!" Harper cried out, reaching for Brodie again.

"Run, Harper!" Brodie shouted. "Take the zip line across the cove! It's the one place they told us to stay away from, so it may be a way out!"

Harper observed the distressed look in Director McGee's eyes and realized that Brodie might be right. But she couldn't just leave Brodie to die.

"I'm not going without you!" she said.

"Please! You're our only hope," Brodie urged, just before Counselor Fuller waved her hand over his mouth and used her ghost powers to magically seal his lips.

Harper knew Brodie was right. Her escaping and getting help was their only chance.

She turned and ran as fast as she could into the thick, swirling mist.

Toward the cove.

When she looked back over her shoulder, she heard the hair-raising shrill again and saw the two phantom-counselors hover out of the open window. . . .

And their eyes were glowing bright as spotlights.

# 18

# PORTAL

**H**arper sprinted into the unknown. The fog wrapped around her like a blanket, absorbing her deeper into its mystery.

She felt lost, afraid, desperate.

When she arrived at the muddy bank, she stopped and stared out at the water. The surface was still, like a haunted mirror. The mist hovering over it seemed to be waiting for her. Beckoning her into its secrets.

The ladder to the zip-line platform stood before her, still covered in yellow caution tape. Harper glanced up, able to see only five or ten feet up the ladder. Whatever was above was completely hidden.

Sensing that Director McGee and Counselor Fuller would be there soon, she glanced back toward camp. She expected to see them floating in her direction. But they were nowhere in sight.

Remembering Brodie's last words, Harper began to climb the ladder, one rung at a time.

She felt like she was being swallowed by a cloud. Soon, she no longer saw the ground beneath her, nor could she see anything above. All she could do was trust that the ladder would lead her to escape.

*What if there's nothing up here? What if there's no zip line at all?*

The thought disturbed her. But it didn't slow her down.

Soon, she arrived at a wooden platform with an entry hole carved out of the middle of it. She climbed through it and was relieved that the zip line was actually there, just like the counselors had said. But there was something else there too.

A metal rod.

With a blinking light attached to it.

Pointed toward the sky.

*This must be a cell tower,* Harper thought. *They were lying the whole time about not having cell service this far into the woods. But why would ghosts need a cell tower?*

She then stepped to the edge of the platform. The mini trapeze bar was made of metal, and the thick wire disappeared into the mist above the lake. She couldn't help but wonder if it led to safety or to certain death.

Without time to think, she tucked her flashlight in her back pocket, grabbed hold of the trapeze handle, and pushed off into the unknown.

There was a loud hissing above her as the wheel joint rolled over the metal wire. Harper soared through the mist, feeling something she had never felt before, even in dreams.

She was moving so fast, she felt like she was flying.

*Maybe I'll escape them after all,* she thought.

But then . . .

She saw the ground on the other side of the lake.

Coming closer.

And closer.

*Where is the brake on this thing?* she wondered in a panic.

A second later, Harper crashed hard, tumbling to the ground. She stood and brushed herself off.

But when she looked up, she froze.

There, in the eerie night forest, was . . .

A gang of ghosts. Waiting for her in the fog ahead.

Terror rushed through her.

She had nowhere to run.

Nowhere to hide.

And then . . .

She squinted and realized they weren't ghosts. But they were almost as spooky.

"Gravestones," she whispered.

There were dozens of them.

The deteriorating markers rose from the

ground like cracked teeth.

*This must be part of the graveyard the camp-ground was built on top of,* she thought.

The fog crept through the wooded cemetery, slithering in and out between the tombstones and trees.

Another uncomfortable thought soon struck Harper. *Maybe this is where Director McGee's and Counselor Fuller's bodies are buried—if those are even their real names. If I can find their graves, maybe I can find a way to stop them from taking the kids to the ghost world.*

Harper began searching the faces of the stones for the names of the counselors. She shined her flashlight at each one, even tracing her finger over the letters. But most of the words were too faded to read.

Then she noticed newer tombstones, ones with names and strange symbols that had been freshly carved into them.

She read one.

Then another.

And another.

She couldn't help but think that the names sounded familiar.

Like they were people she knew.

And that's when she saw something even more petrifying.

There, on the one right in front of her, was . . .

Her own name.

She blinked and read it again, hoping her eyes were playing tricks on her.

But there it was. Her first and last name.

Clear as day.

Strangely, there was no birth or death date listed.

That's when it hit her that all the names on the newer tombstones were the names of the campers she had met during the week.

*Did they kill all the campers and bury them here?* she thought. *And is this where they're planning to bury me?*

She frantically searched for Darla's and Regina's names to see if their bodies were there. But the graves by their names had yet to be filled—they were still hollow.

And that's when a series of horrifying realizations invaded her thoughts. . . .

The photos of Bronson McGee going back generations.

Harper not remembering ever actually getting on the bus back in town but simply waking up in the fog.

And how no parents had shown up to pick up a single camper.

*Am I . . . dead?* she wondered.

She looked down at her hands and reached up and touched her face. She couldn't tell if she was dead or alive.

Right then, she saw something just beyond the graveyard.

A flickering light.

And it looked like it was coming from another dimension.

# 19

# COCOONS

**H**arper stepped toward the light and realized it was coming from a cave. Its dark mouth was a perfect arch carved into the side of a dome-like hill covered in brush and rocks.

She debated whether to find a path away from camp, but something kept pulling her toward the light, like a magnet.

One step.

Two steps.

Three steps.

She was no longer in control of her body. It was moving without any instructions from her mind.

As she was lured closer to the cave, she was struck by an epiphany.

*The fog's not coming from the sky,* she realized. *It's coming from this cave.*

She watched as an endless cloud of mist flooded out and into the forest beyond it. The pulsing light was coming from somewhere deep inside the cave. It glowed blue, like light beneath water. It was dazzling, even hypnotic.

But what was its source?

Harper took a deep breath and entered the cave, unsure what lay ahead. She wanted to know exactly where the fog was coming from. And why.

She thought of everything she had seen, everything that had happened, since she had arrived at Camp Moon Lake. . . .

Regina's cruelty to Darla. Darla's evil smile of revenge. The green slime. The disappearing campers. The light beams above the cove. Escaping camp and showing up right back at its doorstep.

She had thought she was coming to the most

magical summer camp on earth. A place of fun and wonder. But she had met so much darkness. And now she was all alone.

A few steps into the cave, a horrible smell filled her nostrils.

Then something dripped on her arm.

She looked down at her skin and saw . . .

Green slime.

The same glowing ooze she had seen on Darla's glasses and on Regina's bunk bed.

"Yuck!" she said.

Harper wiped the slime off on her shorts, then looked up and saw something even more grotesque attached to the walls of the cave. . . .

Giant.

Slimy.

Cocoons.

Dozens of them.

They were all attached to the walls and ceiling with a sticky web of slime.

*So it was real slime after all*, she thought.

Then she saw something else that made her stomach churn. . . .

A face.

Inside one of the cocoons.

And whoever was in there was still breath-ing.

*The campers*, she thought.

She hurried over to the cocoon and peered at the face inside.

"Regina," Harper whispered in disbelief.

She quickly clawed away the slime covering Regina's face. It felt like the goo that came out of the quarter machine at the pizza parlor back home. As soon as Harper had removed enough of it, Regina gasped for breath.

Harper tore at the meringue-like cover-ing on the rest of Regina's body, then carefully laid Regina on the ground to give her room to breathe.

The captive girl fought to open her eyes. At the sight of Harper, she tried to move her lips to speak.

That's when Regina spoke a single word that filled Harper with dread. . . .

"RUN!"

Harper's heart pounded in her chest. Her breath quickened.

She looked out the mouth of the cave and saw a dozen glowing eyes floating through the forest. Hunting for her.

*The ghost counselors are almost here!* she thought.

Quickly, she hid Regina behind a nearby boulder and scavenged for a place to hide. But the only way open to her was farther into the dark throat of the cave.

Harper stood immobilized. She tried to move her legs, but fear had turned them to stone.

Director McGee, Counselor Fuller, and the rest of the ghost counselors entered the cave and hovered toward her. She was shocked to see that Nurse Betty and the bus driver were there too.

Even though the light from their eyes was near blinding, Harper could see that they were holding something. . . .

"Brodie," she whispered.

His eyes were closed, and he looked

unconscious. Even worse, his skin was paler than usual, like he had lost circulation. He seemed frozen inside some otherworldly spell. Harper was glad that he was still in one piece, but she was terrified of what they would do with him.

"Why are you doing this?" she asked Director McGee while holding back tears.

Director McGee hovered toward her and stopped a few inches in front of her face.

Then he said something that obliterated every suspicion she had entertained.

"Snacks," he said. "We need snacks."

What he did next was so unexpected, so terrible, that even Brodie couldn't have dreamed up the twist. . . .

# 20

# JUNK FOOD

**H**arper watched in horror as Director McGee reached to the back of his neck and unzipped his skin.

Counselor Fuller did the same.

And all the other counselors did too.

They tossed their human suits to the ground. The eyeless masks and heaps of skin lying in a pile looked so creepy, so impossible.

Harper nearly fainted from fright.

Their natural bodies weren't like anything she had ever seen. Their real skin was green and slimy, and they could mold themselves into any shape as if they were made of Play-Doh.

It was then that Harper realized they weren't ghosts.

They were something else entirely.

She recalled the strange symbols on the tombstones and the odd language she had heard Director McGee and Counselor Fuller speaking at one point during their conversation by the fireplace. Then she remembered what they had said about taking campers to the next world.

That's when it hit her. . . .

*Impossible*, she thought. *They're . . . ALIENS!*

The truth blew her mind like a nuclear explosion.

She watched in horror as the extraterrestrials' drooling mouths moved, and the antennas on the tops of their heads seemed to translate: "It's time for you to take the next step."

"Next step?" Harper asked, trembling with fear.

"Food preparation," the creature that was Counselor Fuller answered, nodding toward the cocoons on the walls. "Earth is just a brief stop on our journey. We needed to refuel and get more snacks to last us until we arrive at the next planetary system that harbors edible life. The cocoons are seasoning the specimens as we speak, and we'll soon transfer them to their individually marked freezers for food preservation."

She pointed toward the gravestones outside the cave, and Harper realized that they weren't tombstones. . . . They were name markers for some kind of underground cryogenic freezer.

Her head spun with questions. "You mean that Earth . . . is like a gas station on an intergalactic road trip?" she asked, remembering her dad pulling over to get gas and snacks on their family vacation earlier that summer.

"Exactly," Counselor Fuller communicated through her antennas. "We've been fattening you up with the junk food of your planet so that you can be *our* junk food."

*A twist on a twist*, Harper thought, wishing Brodie was awake to hear it.

Horrified, she took a step back.

Just then, the alien that was Director McGee hovered toward her. . . .

"For a hundred years, I've managed the operation on this planet," he revealed. "Some of the 'counselors,' like myself, stay on Earth long term, sending out brochures, conducting the phone interviews with potential campers, informing human families that their kids have been chosen to come to Camp Moon Lake. Finally, I'll be retiring after this week, and Counselor Fuller will be taking my place."

Harper glanced at Counselor Fuller, who was now a giant green blob. Harper had trusted her entirely, but she now knew without a doubt that her instincts had been wrong.

"What about the parents of the kids you take?" Harper asked, her voice trembling. "Surely they would have exposed the camp by now."

Director McGee shook his blobby head. "Our planetary agents swipe the minds of everyone who's ever known or heard of our campers. The agents go into neighborhoods, schools, bedrooms, and extinguish all recollections and remnants. We leave no trace behind. It's as if the campers never existed."

Harper shivered at the horrifying idea of being erased from her parents' minds. "Why don't you take adults instead? They're bigger, and th-there's more meat on them," Harper said.

"Human children are a delicacy, whereas adults are rather . . . tasteless. Besides, we need to leave the adults behind in order for them to continue growing the population. Which means more snacks for us. It's better if we let things take their natural course, and we harvest in secret. All the stories of alien abductions you hear about in the news and tabloids—they're all true. But those stories usually come out because one of our agents didn't follow protocol."

"So Camp Moon Lake is all just a big ruse? That's why you keep everything a secret here?" she asked.

Director McGee nodded. "In the old days it was easy to keep the secrets of camp, but it's gotten much harder in recent years with your species discovering more advanced technologies. Smartphones that take pictures and videos that can be instantaneously sent back to your families and friends. We've had to crack down on these things in order to preserve our cover."

He moved toward Harper, and she took another step back.

She could tell she was running out of options.

"Don't worry, though," Director McGee said. "It will all be over soon. I promise you won't feel a thing."

He moved toward her again, and she felt all the muscles in her body tense.

Harper turned and sprinted out of the circle of aliens and deeper into the rocky tunnel, hoping she could find another way out.

"There's no use running!" Director McGee called after her. "You can't escape!"

But Harper only ran faster. She traveled deeper and deeper into the cave, passing beneath the canopy of cocoons.

All the while, she followed the eerie blue

light up ahead. It was the same pulsing light she had seen from outside the cave.

As she drew closer, she realized that it was coming from a giant metal box. A machine of some kind.

The contraption had long translucent tentacles that were planted into the ground. It seemed to be sucking up natural resources—soil, minerals, and water—from beneath the surface.

But most intriguing of all . . .

It was pumping an enormous amount of exhaust into the atmosphere.

*This is where the fog has been coming from the whole time!* Harper realized. *But . . . what is this machine doing?*

She examined it for a moment and deduced that it was somehow connected to the floor of the cave through a network of wires. She glanced around at the ceiling, the ground, and the walls covered with cocoons. Then she saw what looked like tinted windows—the kind you'd find in an airplane. But they looked camouflaged.

That's when she realized she wasn't standing in a cave at all. . . .

She was trapped inside the belly of the aliens' spaceship.

# 21

# A TWIST ON A TWIST

*This has to be a nightmare,* she thought. *At any moment, I'll wake up, and I'll be back home. And Mom will have breakfast ready downstairs.*

She pinched herself, hoping to wake up. But she remained in the belly of the spaceship.

There was a mustardy odor in the air. The sour scent made her cringe. She suspected it was a stench the aliens had brought from their home planet.

Just as she was about to turn around, someone grabbed her shoulder.

"Ahh!" she screamed, raising her fist.

It was Brodie.

He looked just as afraid as she was.

"How did you escape? I figured you'd be marinating in a cocoon by now!" she said, then hugged him.

"I pretended to be unconscious and slipped away when they weren't looking," Brodie replied.

At the sight of him, Harper felt renewed hope. At the very least, she reasoned, if she was going to die, she wouldn't have to do it alone.

"The counselors are aliens," she said. "We're inside their spaceship right now. We have to find a way out quick, or else they're going to eat all of us!"

"I know. I heard them talking," Brodie replied, almost as if he was more amused than afraid. "It's like *Stranger Things* meets *Close Encounters of the Third Kind*. The good thing is that these aliens move slower than us, so we have an advantage. But I've already looked everywhere. The only way out is the way we came in."

He pointed over his shoulder in the direction of what Harper had believed was the mouth of the cave, knowing now that it was really the door to the ship.

"There has to be another exit," she said. "Or if we can find a weak spot somewhere on the ship, maybe we can destroy it. There might even still be a way to save the other campers."

Harper began feeling along the walls, searching for a secret door or access point.

"The only way to do that would be to access the ship's mainframe computer and destroy the antenna that notifies other orbiting ships that the food is prepared," Brodie said. "It's like a lighthouse that alerts them that the snack bar is open here on Earth."

"How in the world would you know that?" Harper asked, fumbling along the walls.

When Brodie didn't answer, she got a churning feeling in her stomach. She slowly turned.

"Because it's the truth," Brodie said, his eyes glazed over, possessed with something dark. "We need you, Harper. We need all of you."

Then . . .

He reached to the back of his neck and began to unzip his human suit.

# 22

# THE THING ABOUT HOPE

**B**rodie threw his skin on the ground beside him. His gooey, green body wobbled as he hovered in midair. He looked disgusting, and from his moldy appearance, Harper wondered if he might be a thousand years old.

"Y-you've been one of them all along?" Harper asked, her voice shaking, realizing that she had no one left to trust. She did everything she could to hold back tears.

"I was assigned to keep an eye on you to make sure you'd be ready," Brodie communicated through his antennas.

"Ready for what?"

Brodie hovered toward her. "To be my snack."

The hairs on Harper's arm raised, and she took a step back.

"The truth was right in front of you the whole time. But you humans are far too trusting," Brodie continued. "And you're easy to control when you're afraid."

"So everything's been an illusion? The entire camp was created just to capture human kids to eat on your intergalactic road trips?" she said.

"Yes. Human children are the most vulnerable of your species. But to be fair, we've become masterful actors. While on our way to your planet, Director McGee sent a message to our ship, encouraging us to watch all your movies and TV shows to learn about your kind. Day after day, year after year, your satellites are sending your stories out into the cosmos, exposing yourselves to all intelligent civilizations. You might as well have a bright blinking neon sign posted on your world saying, 'Free food!' We aren't the first to come here, and we certainly won't be the last. But we haven't been thinking big enough. . . . And once my mom takes over, we'll franchise the ruse of Camp Moon Lake to a thousand other planets."

"Your mom?" Harper asked.

"You know her as Counselor Fuller. She has big ideas. Director McGee has always thought too small. And once he's gone, we'll be able to harvest ten times as many humans as before."

Harper couldn't believe what she was hearing. It felt like something out of *The Twilight Zone*.

*No wonder Brodie kept making movie references!* Harper thought. *It's all he knows about Earth.*

Brodie hovered closer to her. "While studying your genetic order, we discovered that out of all the human emotions, fear is the most powerful. If you can make humans afraid, then you can control them. That's why we made up the story about the ghost girl—to keep you away from the cove, away from the truth. As part of the experiment, I even gave you a hint early on when I made up the story about the camp murders and then revealed that it was a lie. You should have known then not to trust me, but your desire to believe in me was your weakness."

Harper thought of the politicians, world leaders, and all the crazy images her dad watched on the evening news. She suspected Brodie might be right. But then she felt something deep inside her that contradicted what she was thinking.

"Y-you're wrong about one thing," she stuttered, trying to maintain her poise.

"And what's that?" Brodie asked.

"There's something stronger than fear," she challenged, then took a step toward him, boldly. "Courage."

In response, Brodie's antennas began to make a laughing noise. He opened his mouth, revealing hundreds of sharklike teeth. To Harper's surprise, out of his throat came a shrill noise that sounded like it was spilling out from the blackest void in the universe. It was the same sound she had heard coming from the cove.

The breath in Harper's lungs extinguished like a candle flame turning to darkness.

In a panic, she again felt around on the wall behind her. She knew her chances of escape were slim at this point, but she had to keep trying.

Brodie floated around her, like a beast circling its prey.

But then Harper heard a voice. . . .

And it was coming from inside her own head.

"Harper, it's me. Regina."

*Regina?* Harper thought.

"Yeah, I'm using this weird telepathic audio device I found in their control room. It's letting me talk inside your mind."

*What?*

"Just trust me. In a few seconds, I'm going to open a secret passageway behind you. I can see it on the video feed right now. But you have to jump through it right away so I can close it before Brodie gets to you."

*Nuh-uh. No way. I saw what you did to Darla on the trust fall.*

"This is different. I promise I'll catch you."

*How do I know you're not one of them and this isn't just part of the trap?*

"Because I was in a cocoon! Tabitha's one of them, and she tricked me into sneaking out of the cabin one night and then put me in there."

*You could just be making that up. Your name wasn't on the camper list!*

"Probably because it was a list of the alien campers. I'm human—I promise."

*But how can I know for sure?*

"You'll just have to weigh your options. But hurry—you don't have much time. Five, four, three, two, one . . ."

Right then, a door in the wall behind Harper opened, and she glanced down into the black void. It looked like a death sentence. But she didn't have much choice. She could either stay and be Brodie's snack or take her chances with Regina.

So she took her chances and stepped through the doorway.

Brodie rushed after her, but the door closed just in time to seal him off.

Harper tumbled down the chamber between the walls, and her body banged around like she was a rag doll. Finally, she landed in Regina's arms.

"How did you escape?" Harper asked, standing to her feet.

"I crawled along the wall and fell into some kind of vacuum chute. I ended up here and saw you on the video feed," Regina explained, pointing to the video monitors on the nearby wall. "I swear, my dad's made me watch *E.T.* like twenty times, and I thought aliens were supposed to be nice!"

"Thanks for saving me," Harper said, then glanced around at the dim chamber. It was round and had an arched ceiling. She figured the entire room was half the size of a basketball court.

"Hey, you saved me first," Regina said. "As far as I can tell, this must be the mainframe of the Mother Ship. We better hurry. I'm sure they'll find us soon."

Harper suddenly felt a surge of hope.

"Brodie said something about an antenna that alerts alien ships that the earth food is ready," she said. "If we can figure out a way to destroy it, maybe we can stop the operation once and for all."

Regina pointed to one of a dozen video monitors. "Is that the antenna you're talking about?"

Harper saw a live feed of the top of the zipline platform. There was the cell tower, with its blinking light.

"That's it!" Harper said. "I thought it was a cell tower, but it's their antenna!"

Regina immediately went to the computer keyboard, which was made of strange holographic symbols that hovered midair. She examined it for a moment, then began typing away.

"How do you know what you're doing?" Harper asked, starting to feel suspicious again.

"These computers run on a simpler code than you think," Regina said.

Harper stared at her blankly.

"I'm three-time state champion at robotics

and computer coding," Regina said. "How do you think I have so many Instagram followers? I know all the algorithms. You probably thought I was a cheerleader or something."

*Regina's a computer wiz?* Harper thought in astonishment.

Regina's hands moved across the keys like she was conducting a symphony, conjuring secret music beyond Harper's comprehension.

Finally, the lighthouse antenna on the video screen went dark.

"There, I did it!" Regina said. "Now, if I can find an emergency exit so we can get out of here . . ."

Regina squinted, examining the buttons again. She looked up at the video feed of the cocoons, then back to the buttons. "I think I have an idea," she said. Then she pressed the keys like a madwoman, as if she was typing a novel.

Suddenly, the light in the room turned bright red, and a sharp beeping sound began to shriek from the communication system overhead.

"What did you do?" Harper asked.

But Regina didn't answer.

They waited.

And waited.

But nothing happened.

Slowly, Harper accepted the truth. . . .

They were trapped. With no way out.

# 23

## ESCAPE

Just then, they heard an unexpected sound. . . .

Laughter.

Harper turned and saw the entire army of aliens entering through a door on the other side of the chamber, invading the mission control room.

They circled around Harper and Regina, closing in tight so that they couldn't run away this time. At the sight of the silvery drool dripping from their rubbery lips, Harper and Regina backed up against the massive frame of the supercomputer.

Director McGee and Counselor Fuller were at the front.

"I told you it's no use trying to escape," Director McGee said with a sinister chuckle. "But thanks for activating the release of the cocoons so that we can transfer the kids to the freezer. You've helped us with the next stage of our plan."

Harper looked at Regina. "Did you mean to do that?"

Regina didn't reply.

Director McGee moved toward them like a levitating snail. Slime dripped from his swollen body onto the sleek black floor, then evaporated. As if by magic.

"Let me take care of them," Counselor Fuller said, shoving her way in front of him.

"Must I remind you that I'm still the director of this operation?" Director McGee replied crossly.

"But not for much longer," Counselor Fuller said. "Technically, my appointment begins today."

Director McGee and Counselor Fuller

turned and faced each other, then began arguing.

Harper reexamined her and Regina's situation. After a moment, she leaned over to Regina and whispered, "See that blue button over there?" Regina nodded. "You push that one, and I'll push this one over here. I think they might open a door or something. But the aliens must use their tentacles to reach them, so you and I will have to push them at the same time."

Regina inspected the buttons. "I'm eighty-seven percent sure this could end badly."

"You have a better idea?"

"No," Regina replied. "Ready?"

Harper nodded. But just before she pushed the button next to her, a thought caused her to hesitate. "What about the other campers?"

"They'll be fine. Trust me," Regina said. Without another moment to waste, they began to count down together.

"Three, two, one . . ."

At the same time, Harper and Regina pounded their fists against the blue buttons, and the buttons turned red.

"Stop that!" Director McGee shouted at Harper and Regina, distracted from his confrontation with Counselor Fuller.

Right then, the alarm on the communication system stopped beeping.

It was silent for a moment, then . . .

It started shrieking like a siren. This time louder and faster.

Director McGee's antennas perked at the enhanced alarm, and his eyes grew wide. His head spun around on his body as he glanced at the video feed of the mysterious machine that had been extracting earth's resources in the tunnel. The machine's exhaust, the fog, was beginning to thin out.

He jerked back toward Harper.

"The fuel system is stopping. What have you done?"

"I—I don't know," Harper said.

She suddenly realized that the machine in the tunnel was harvesting resources from the Earth in order to power the spaceship. The contraption was like a gas pump at a corner store. It was the source of their fuel!

Before Harper could say anything else, a robotic voice sounded over the intercom system throughout the entire ship. "Attention, fellow Weebonites. Liftoff has been activated, which means our mission here is complete. At the conclusion of this message, you will have exactly three minutes to secure yourself before ascension. It will then be seven hundred and forty-two Earth years until we arrive at Planet Xultron for our next snack break on the Intergalactic Tour. The sleep-inducing fumes will begin now. Sit back, relax, and enjoy your trip."

*Liftoff?!* Harper thought in horror.

Right then, the vents above hissed, and a purple mist puffed out of them, traveling toward the aliens' reptilian nostrils.

Panic surged through Harper's body. Not only was she surrounded by ravenous aliens, but now there was a clock ticking down to when the ship would leave Earth and carry her off into outer space to be eaten alive.

Just then, the ship vibrated. And the voice on the intercom began to count down.

As if things couldn't get any worse, Harper glanced over and saw Regina's eyes beginning to close. . . . The computer whiz—her only hope—was losing consciousness.

# 24
# ESCAPE

Regina was fading fast. Harper lightly slapped her cheeks, trying to keep her awake. All the while, she covered her own mouth and nose with her shirt.

At the sound of the robotic voice counting down, the aliens' hollow eyes grew wide. Their skin turned yellow with fear. And their antennas buzzed with panic.

Harper's vision began to blur as well, and she knew she had to find a way out of the ship immediately, or else she'd be cruising across the galaxy in less than three minutes.

*Regina said she came here through a chute that led down from the cocoon chamber to this room,* she thought. *If I can find it, maybe I can get back to the entrance.*

Harper watched as the flustered extraterrestrials scrambled out of doors, into secret rooms, and to various command stations, to strap themselves into the Mother Ship. The whole scene looked like an ant pile that had been sprayed with insecticide.

It wasn't long before she saw Director McGee and Counselor Fuller sit down at an opening in the wall, pull a small lever, and ascend out of sight.

*That must be the chute that leads back to the entrance!*

Harper hurried over and sat herself and Regina down at the edge of the portal. She pulled the lever next to her, and a vacuum force shot them upward like on an antigravity slide.

Once they were out of the fumes, Regina regained consciousness and opened her eyes. Harper helped her to her feet.

They both looked around in shock.

The cocoons had already melted from the walls. There were gooey piles of mush everywhere on the ground, where Harper expected to see disoriented campers. But there were none in sight.

"They must have already transferred the kids to the freezers," Harper said with a pang in her stomach.

"We—have—to—hurry," Regina reminded her.

Together they ran toward the entrance and out the door of the ship.

With less than thirty seconds left in the countdown, Harper and Regina hid behind some nearby bushes.

But before Harper had time to breathe a sigh of relief, she saw one camper still inside the ship.

"Darla," she whispered, glad to see her still alive.

The bewildered girl looked distraught, staring down at the abandoned human suits lying in a pile on the ground. Several aliens were hovering toward her with their antennas outstretched.

Instinctively, Harper ran back inside the ship and grabbed Darla's arm. "We have to get out of here, Darla! Now!"

She tugged Darla toward the open exit. Still disoriented, Darla tried to pull away from Harper, but Harper dragged her out of the tunnel and onto the forest ground just as the cosmic door of the spaceship closed.

A jetlike roar reverberated from the ship. It sounded like a SpaceX rocket about to launch.

Harper, Darla, and Regina watched with mouths agape as the Mother Ship lifted off the ground, tearing away the surface of the earth that had grown on top of it.

The camouflage of dirt and trees and rocks slid off the ship, revealing a giant silver disc with tiny black windows all around its perimeter. Harper had never seen anything like it. And she wondered exactly how long it had been hiding there in the forest.

The flying saucer hovered there for a moment, making an eerie humming sound.

Slowly, the name markers she had thought had been tombstones but were really individualized cubbies for the aliens' freezer folded up into the ship like drawers into a wardrobe. Harper had a terrible, helpless feeling at the realization that all the campers were inside them and that they'd soon be turned into snacks!

Then . . .

A loud sonic boom shook her ears, and the ship shot up into the sky, as if on an invisible track, and disappeared into outer space.

In a blink, it was gone, like a nightmare where only the icky residue of the memory remains.

As soon as it was out of sight, the fog in the forest began to dissipate. The serene sounds of nature invaded Harper's ears. She could hear the owls, the birds, the creaking trees, even the soothing whisper of water washing up against the shore of the nearby lake.

*All the campers—they're gone*, she thought,

tears forming in her eyes. It was the saddest feeling she had ever felt—even sadder than the thought of her parents splitting up.

But then . . .

She saw a face appear behind a nearby bush.

And another.

And another.

Until she saw the eyes of dozens of kids hiding there.

"The campers," Harper whispered, hardly believing her eyes. "But how?"

Regina cleared her throat.

"I reprogrammed the transfer so that the ship's mechanical arms moved the cocoons to behind those bushes instead of into the freezers," Regina said with a smile. "And I also erased Earth from the ship's mapping software. With the antenna down, their operation is ruined."

"Brilliant," Harper said, and patted Regina's shoulder.

All the campers walked out from their hiding places and joined them.

Together they peered up and saw the stars

for the first time all week. Harper knew the sun would be rising soon. And a new day would begin.

Relieved, she took a deep breath and let it out slowly, thinking of all that she had lived through. All that she had survived.

*We beat it*, she thought. *We're alive.*

# 25

# GOODBYES

Later that morning, Harper stood waiting in the same spot where the bus had dropped her off nearly a week before. One of the campers broke into the lock box that held all the cell phones in Director McGee's office, and so everyone was able to call their parents. Cell service worked that far into the woods after all.

Happy to be alive, Harper let several younger campers use her cell phone first, then she called her parents. She couldn't wait for them to get there. There was so much to talk about.

By noon, most of the campers had been

picked up. Harper, Regina, and Darla were the last ones left.

Darla was sitting by herself nearby, quietly contemplating everything that had happened. Harper and Regina sat in the shade of a tree.

"I—I just wanted to say thank you," Regina said. "For saving me—twice. If you hadn't gotten me out of that cocoon, and then out of those fumes, I'd be someone's breakfast right about now."

"Hey, we saved each other," Harper replied. "I would have been eaten alive by Brodie if it weren't for that impromptu trust fall and your wizardly computer skills."

Regina laughed. "You know, no one's ever going to believe us," she said.

"I'm kind of okay with that," Harper replied. "I'd like to forget the whole thing ever happened."

Regina smirked. Then her eyes grew serious as if she was deep in thought.

"I know it won't make up for the way I was acting, but right before camp, my parents told me they were splitting up," Regina revealed. "That's why I was such a bully. I was scared and feeling sort of angry and alone. Anyway, when I called my dad a little while ago, he said that he and mom are going to try to work things out. So I get to go home today."

Harper smiled. "I'm glad your parents decided to work things out. It gives me some hope that maybe mine can too."

Regina returned a half smile. "Yeah, the threat of an alien abduction sort of puts things in perspective."

"You can say that again," Harper said with a chuckle.

"Hey, we should trade numbers," Regina suggested.

Harper took a pen and piece of paper from her backpack. She wrote down her phone number and handed it to Regina, who put the folded paper in her back pocket.

Just then, a black Lexus SUV pulled up.

"Those are my parents," Regina said. "Good luck, Harper. I'll text you soon. And maybe we can even sign up for the same camp next summer."

"Are you kidding? I'm never going to another summer camp for as long as I live," Harper replied, half-joking, half-serious. "But let's definitely stay in touch."

Regina smiled.

Harper watched as she picked up her luggage, then approached Darla, who was sitting on the ground beside her backpack and sleeping bag, staring at the sky.

"Here," Regina said, handing Darla's taped-up glasses to her. "I found these in the forest after the ship took off, and I fixed them for you. I'm really sorry for being so mean. I wish I could take it all back. Anyway, I hope you enjoy the rest of the summer with your family."

Before Darla could respond, Regina disappeared into the Lexus and rode away.

Strangely, as soon as she was out of sight, Darla began to cry.

Harper went and sat beside her.

"You okay? That was just Regina's way of

saying she's sorry," Harper said, patting Darla's back.

Darla looked up through her tears, and for the first time, Harper noticed the fluorescent green color in Darla's eyes.

"You two ruined everything," Darla sniveled. "My family will never come back for me now."

"What are you talking about?" Harper asked. "We saved you."

She didn't know why, but her instincts told her to back away from Darla.

"Maybe they'll come back for me if I send them a signal to let them know all the snacks didn't get away," Darla said, holding up a small alien beacon crowned by an antenna. Then she gripped Harper's forearm tight as a wrench and whispered, "I still have one left."

# ACKNOWLEDGMENTS

"I am a part of all that I have met."
—Alfred, Lord Tennyson

There are quite a few people to acknowledge here in this book of the Monsterstreet series:

First of all, my Mom, Dad, Sis—everything I am is because of you, and words can never express the depth of my gratefulness. I can only hope to honor you with the life I live and the works I create.

All my family: Granddad, Grandmom, Pappa Hugg, Mamma Hugg, Lilla, Meemaw, Nanny, GG, Grandmother Hugghins, Marilyn, Steve, Haddie, Jude, Beckett, Uncle Hal, Aunt Cathy, Nicole, Dylan, Aunt Rhonda, Uncle Greg,

Sam, Jake, Trey, Uncle Johnny, Aunt Glynis, Jerod, Chad, Aunt Jodie, Uncle Terry, Natalie, Mitchell, Anna, David, Hannah, David Nevin, Joy, Lukas, Teresa, and Aunt Jan.

Teachers, coaches, mentors, colleagues, and students: Jeanie Johnson, David Vardeman, Pat Vaughn, Lee Carter, Robert Darden, Kevin Reynolds, Ray Bradbury, R.L. Stine, Rikki Coke (Wiethorn), Peggy Jezek, Kathi Couch, Jill Osborne Wilkinson, Marla Jaynes, Karen Deaconson, Su Milam, Karen Copeland, Corrie Dixon, Nancy Evans Hutto, Pam Dominik, Jean Garner, Randy Crawford, Pat Zachry, Eddie Sherman, Scott Copeland, Heidi Kunkel, Brian Boyd, Sherry Rogers, Lisa Osborne, Wes Evans, Betsy Barry, Karen Hix, Sherron Boyd, Mrs. Kahn, Mrs. Turk, Mrs. Schroeder, Mrs. Battle, Mrs. McCracken, Nancy Frame Chiles, Mrs. Adkins, Kim Pearson, Mrs. Harvey, Elaine Spence, Barbara Fulmer, Julie Schrotel, Barbara Belk, Mrs. Reynolds, Vanessa Diffenbaugh, Elisabeth McKetta, Bryan Delaney, Talaya Delaney, Wendy Allman, John Belew,

Vicki Klaras, Gery Greer and Bob Ruddick, Greg Garrett, Chris Seay, Sealy and Matt Yates, David Crowder, Cecile Goyette, Kirby Kim, Mike Simpson, Quinlan Lee, Clay Butler, Mary Darden, Derek Smith, Brian Elliot, Rachel Moore, Naymond Keathley, Steve Sadler, Jimmy and Janet Dorrell, Glenn Blalock, Katie Cook, SJ Murray, Greg Chan, Lorri Shackelford, Tim Fleischer, Byron Weathersbee, Chuck Walker, John Durham, Ron Durham, Bob Johns, Kyle Lake, Kevin Roe, Barby Williams, Nancy Parrish, Joani Livingston, Madeleine Barnett, Diane McDaniel, Beth Hair, Laura Cubos, Sarah Holland, Christe Hancock, Cheryl Cooper, Jeni Smith, Traci Marlin, Jeremy Ferrerro, Maurice and Gloria Walker, Charlotte McDonald, Dana Gietzen, Leighanne Parrish, Heather Helton, Corrie Cubos, all the librarians, teachers, secretaries, students, custodians, and principals at Midway ISD, Waco ISD, Riesel ISD, and Connally ISD, all my apprentices at Moonsung Writing Camp and Camp Imagination, and to my hometown community of Woodway, Texas.

Friends and collaborators: Nathan "Waylon" Jennings, Craig Cunningham, Blake Graham, Susannah Lipsey, Hallie Day, Ali Rodman Wallace, Jered Wilkerson, Brian McDaniel, Meghan Stanley Lynd, Suzanne Hoag Steece, the Jennings family, the Rodman family, the Carter family, all the families of the "Red River Gang," the Cackleberries, the Geib family, Neva Walker and family, Rinky and Hugh Sanders, Clay Rodman, Steven Fischer, Dustin Boyd, Jeff Vander Woude, Randy Stephens, Allen Ferguson, Scott Lynd, Josh Zachry, Scott Crawford, Jourdan Gibson Stewart, Crystal Carter, Kristi Kangas Miller, Taylor Christian, Deanna Dyer Williams, Matt Jennings, Laurie McCool Henderson, Trey Witcher, Genny Pattillo Davis, Brady Williams, Brook Williams Henry, Michael Henry, Jamie Jennings, Jordan Jones, Adrianna Bell Walker, Sarah Rogers Combs, Kayleigh Cunningham, Rich and Megan Roush, Adam Chop, Kimberly Garth Batson, Luke Stanton, Kevin Brown, Britt Knighton, George Cowden, Jenny and Ryan Jamison, Julie Hamilton, Kyle and Emily

Knighton, Ray Small, Jeremy Combs, Mike Trozzo, Allan Marshall, Coleman Hampton, Kent Rabalais, Laura Aldridge, Mikel Hatfield Porter, Edith Reitmeier, Ben Geib, Ashley Vandiver Dalton, Tamarah Johnson, Amanda Hutchison Thompson, Morgan McKenzie Williams, Robbie Phillips, Shane Wilson, J.R. Fleming, Andy Dollerson, Terry Anderson, Mary Anzalone, Chris Ermoian, Chris Erlanson, Greg Peters, Doreen Ravenscroft, Brooke Larue Miceli, Emily Spradling Freeman, Brittany Braden Rowan, Kim Evans Young, Kellis Gilleland Webb, Lindsay Crawford, April Carroll Mureen, Rebekah Croft Georges, Amanda Finnell Brown, Kristen Rash Di Campli, Clint Sherman, Big Shane Smith, Little Shane Smith, Allen Childs, Brandon Hodges, Justin Martin, Eric Lovett, Cody Fredenberg, Tierre Simmons, Bear King, Brady Lillard, Charlie Collier, Aaron Hattier, Keith Jordan, Greg Weghorst, Seth Payne, BJ Carr, Andria Mullins Scarbrough, Lindsey Kelley Palumbo, Cayce Connell Bellinger, David Maness, Ryan

Smith, Marc Uptmore, Kelly Maddux McCarver, Robyn Klatt Areheart, Emily Hoyt Crew, Matt Etter, Logan Walter, Jessica Talley, JT Carpenter, Ryan Michaelis, Audrey Malone Andrews, Amy Achor Blankson, Chad Conine, Hart Robinson, Wade Washmon, Clay Gibson, Barrett Hall, Chad Lemons, Les Strech, Marcus Dracos, Tyler Ellis, Taylor Rudd, James Yarborough, Scott Robison, Bert Vandiver, Clark Richardson, Luke Blount, Allan Gipe, Daniel Fahlenkamp, Ben Hogan, Chris Porter, Reid Johnson, Ryan Stanton, Brian Reis, Ty Sprague, Eric Ellis, Jeremy Gann, Jeff Sadler, Ryan Pryor, Jared Ray, Dustin Dickerson, Reed Collins, Ben Marx, Sammy Rajaratnam, Art Wellborn, Cory Ferguson, Jonathan King, Jim King, Anthony Edwards, Craig Nash, Dillon Meek, Jonathan Stringer, the Bode and Moore families, Jackie and Denver Mills, the Warrior Poets, the Wild Hearts, the Barbaric Yawps, the Bangarang Brothers, and all the Sacred Circle guys (CARPE DIEM).

To all the writers, directors, composers,

producers, artists, creators, inventors, poets, and thinkers who have shaped my life, work, and imagination—a list of luminaries which is far too long to mention here.

To Chris Fenoglio, for creating such stunning covers for the Monsterstreet series. It's safe to say your illustrations pass the ultimate test: they would have made me want to pick up the books when I was a boy! Thank you for lending your incredible talent and imagination to this project.

To the Stimola Literary Studio Family: Erica Rand Silverman, Adriana Stimola, Peter Ryan, Allison Remcheck, and all my fellow authors who are lucky enough to call the Stimola Literary Studio their home.

To the entire HarperCollins publishing family and Katherine Tegen family: Katherine Tegen, David Curtis, Erin Fitzsimmons, Jon Howard, Robby Imfeld, Haley George, and Tanu Srivastava.

To my amazing agent, Rosemary Stimola, who plucked me out of obscurity, remained faithful to this project over the course of not just months but years, and who sets the highest standard of integrity within the wondrous world of children's publishing. I can't tell you how deeply grateful I am for all that you have done for me.

And to my extraordinary editor, Ben Rosenthal. From our very first conversation reminiscing about 1980s movies, I felt in my gut that you were a kindred spirit. Our collaboration on the Monsterstreet series has been one of the greatest joys and adventures of my life, and it's an enormous honor to get to share this journey with you. Thank you for all your guidance, encouragement, and optimism along the way . . . you've been a fantastic captain of this ship!

To my wife and best friend, Rebekah . . . no words can ever tell you how grateful I am for the thousands of hours you've spent reading rough drafts, listening to unpolished ideas, and offering warm, thoughtful encouragement every step of the way. These books wouldn't exist without you, and I'm so glad I get to share this journey and all others by your side.

And lastly, to my most cherished treasures, my precious daughters, Lily Belle and Poet Eve: it is the greatest joy of my life to watch you gaze upon the world with wonder and tell us what you see. May stories always enchant you, and may you grow to tell your own stories someday.